BARBARA CARTLAND'S

Book of

BARBARA CARTLAND'S

Book of Health

JAVELIN BOOKS
POOLE · DORSET

First published in the UK 1985 by Javelin Books,
Link House, West Street, Poole, Dorset, BH15 1LL

British Library Cataloguing in Publication Data

Cartland, Barbara
Barbara Cartland's book of health.
1. Self-care, Health
I. Title
613 RA776.95

ISBN 0 7137 1573 1

Typeset by Colset Private Limited, Singapore

Reproduced, printed and bound in Great Britain by
Hazell Watson & Viney Limited,
Member of the BPCC Group,
Aylesbury, Bucks

CONTENTS

OTHER HEALTH BOOKS BY BARBARA CARTLAND

SOCIOLOGY AND HEALTH

YOU IN THE HOME
THE FASCINATING FORTIES
MARRIAGE FOR MODERNS
BE VIVID, BE VITAL
LOVE, LIFE AND SEX
VITAMINS FOR VITALITY
HUSBANDS AND WIVES
MEN ARE WONDERFUL
ETIQUETTE
THE MANY FACETS OF LOVE
SEX AND THE TEENAGER
THE BOOK OF CHARM
LIVING TOGETHER
THE YOUTH SECRET
THE MAGIC OF HONEY
BOOK OF BEAUTY AND HEALTH
KEEP YOUNG AND BEAUTIFUL (WITH ELINOR GLYNN)
GETTING OLDER, GROWING YOUNGER

COOKERY

BARBARA CARTLAND'S HEALTH FOOD COOKERY BOOK
BARBARA CARTLAND'S FOOD FOR LOVE
BARBARA CARTLAND'S MAGIC OF HONEY COOKBOOK
BARBARA CARTLAND'S RECIPES FOR LOVERS
THE ROMANCE OF FOOD

BARBARA CARTLAND'S EXPERIENCE ON HEALTH

1930–32	Studied Herbal Medicine with the famous Mrs Leyel of Culpeper.
1931–33	A patient and a student of Dr Dengler of Baden-Baden. First use of olive oil as an internal treatment of liver complaints, colitis and inflammation of the bowel.
1930–37	Helped Lady Rhys-Williams giving Vitamin B for habitual abortion and malnutrition in the Distressed Areas.
	Studied the first use of Vitamin E with brood mares and later for barren women.
1935 onwards	Worked with Dr Pierre Lansel, M.D., first Practitioner in England to give injections of Vit. B and C. Followed his experiments with hormones for rejuvenation and the Nieheims treatment of Cell Therapy. Studied with two eminent Doctors the effect of oil injection on external Haemorrhoids.
	Studied the nutritional condition in her brother's Parliamentary Constituency, King's Norton Division of Birmingham, where there was malnutrition from low wages.
	Practised Yoga exercises and breathing with the only white Yogi in the world. Wrote in a monthly magazine on the subject.
	Studied nutrition in Montreal and did two lecture tours in lower Canada during v.hich visited a large number of schools and hospitals.
1939–45	Country Cadet Officer for the St John Ambulance Brigade, Bedfordshire. Arranged First Aid and Home Nursing Lectures and discussed Nutrition with doctors from overseas. Only Honorary Member of

the Officers' Mess (Doctors and Psychiatrists) of 101 Convalescent Home, the largest Rehabilitation Centre in Great Britain.

Looked after 10,000 RAF and the US Flying Fortresses until the American Red Cross arrived.

Studied nutrition of the troops and the conditions in the Prisoner of War Camps.

As Lady County Welfare Officer of Bedfordshire Voluntary Junior Commander (Captain) ATS., dealt with innumerable complaints over food from RAF Camps, Secret Stations and Searchlight Posts and with the health and employment of pregnant mothers from all three Services. Studied conditions in the hospitals treating the women in the Armed Services.

1945 Was introduced in America to the first B-Complex Multi-Vitamin (synthetic) capsule. On return home was closely in touch with the American manufacturers of Vitamins, receiving regular reports, literature and supplies until the Organic Vitamin Company opened at Hemel Hempstead.

1950 Vitamins saved her life. Kept fifty-two farrowing sows on her farm in Hertfordshire and experimented by giving them and the Boars Brewers Yeast from a Brewery. For four years held the record production for Great Britain with an average of eleven a litter. Method copied by Sir Harry Haig for Ovaltine. Her prize-winning bull was given Vitamin E injections.

1955 Published: *Marriage for Moderns, Be Vivid Be Vital, Love, Life and Sex, Vitamins for Vitality*, etc.

Began her lectures on Health.

Became a County Councillor of Hertfordshire, on Education and Health

Committees for nine years.
Studied nutrition with regard to school meals. Deeply concerned with the health and conditions of Old People. Was so horrified at the way they were fed in some Homes, and their general treatment, that her daughter then Viscountess Lewisham visited 250 Homes all over Great Britain.
Following her reports and Barbara Cartland's and the tremendous press publicity involved, the Minister for Housing and Local Government (The Rt Hon Duncan Sandys, MP) instigated an enquiry into the 'Housing and Conditions of the Elderly'.
Was on the Managerial Committee of several Old Peoples Homes and a Patron of Cell Barnes, the largest Home for retarded children in Great Britain.
Visited and inspected innumerable hospitals, clinics and Homes for the Elderly and children. Started her fight for better salaries and conditions for Midwives and Nurses, which brought her into close contact with many of the teaching hospitals and Royal College of Midwives.

1958 Was host to Professor Ana Aslan, founder of H3 on her first visit to England at the invitation of 400 doctors. Also tried Acupuncture and the Cryiac Method of holding a slipped rib or disc.

1960 Started to write monthly for *Here's Health*.
Co-founder of the National Association for Health.
Answered 5,000 letters a year — 10,000 in 1984. *The Magic of Honey* (1 million copies), doubled the sale of honey in Great Britain and over the world.
Lectured on Health to:
The Southgate Technical Colllege
The Queen Elizabeth College of Nutrition

The Polytechnic
The Hertfordshire Police Cadets
Two lectures in the Birmingham Town Hall to audiences of 2,500
Frequent lectures to Midwives, Universities, Rotary Clubs etc.

1964–78 Given a Civic Reception by the Mayor of Vienna for her work in the Health Movement.

Had private discussions on Health, herbs and health foods with:

The Ministers of Health and Sciences in Mexico, Japan and India. Professors and Scientists in Mysore working on the development of agriculture in the famine areas near Kerel with the India Ladies Committee and Officials on Health in Bombay, New Delhi and Mysore.

In touch with the Indian Guild of Service working among orphans, and in the poor areas in India, and saw the conditions among the first three million Pakistanis which moved into Calcutta in 1958.

Visited the new refugee areas in Hong Kong, was the first woman to visit (with the police) the Chinese border seeing the conditions of the workers.

Visited Nepal and saw the insanitary conditions in Katmandu and the rat-infested refuse in the streets. Discussed the conditions with officials.

Visited hospitals, clinics and old people's homes in many parts of India, Bangkok, Hong Kong, Singapore, Switzerland, Austria and France.

Taken on a special visit with five doctors and scientists to inspect the Vitel Clinic in France.

Visited the slums of Delhi, Calcutta, Bombay, Pnompenh (Cambodia), Taiwan,

Singapore, Rio, Harlem (New York), Glasgow, London, and had talks with the leading doctor in Istanbul and was shown Clinical Trials undertaken.

Is closely in touch with the pioneers of the Health Movement in South Africa.

Invited — as a guest — to Yugoslavia, Germany and France.

1978	Visited Leningrad and Moscow and had talks with the Scientists on Old Age problems and the use of Ginseng.
1984	A Dame of Grace of St John of Jerusalem: Chairman of the St John Council, and Deputy President of the St John Ambulance Brigade in Hertfordshire. One of the first women in 1,000 years to be on the Chapter General; President of the Hertfordshire Branch of the Royal College of Midwives: President of the National Association for Health.

ABOUT THE AUTHOR

Barbara Cartland, the world's most famous romantic novelist, who is also an historian, playwright, lecturer, political speaker and television personality, has now written over 390 books and sold over 370 million books over the world.

She has also had many historical works published and has written four autobiographies as well as the biographies of her mother and that of her brother, Ronald Cartland, who was the first Member of Parliament to be killed in the last war. This book has a preface by Sir Winston Churchill and has just been republished with an introduction by Sir Arthur Bryant.

Love at the Helm a novel written with the help and inspiration of the late Earl Mountbatten of Burma, Uncle of His Royal Highness Prince Philip, is being sold for the Mountbatten Memorial Trust.

Miss Cartland in 1978 sang an Album of Love Songs with the Royal Philharmonic Orchestra.

In 1976, by writing twenty-one books, she broke the world record and has continued for the following seven years with 24, 20, 23, 24, 24, 25 and 22. In the *Guinness Book of Records* she is listed as the world's top-selling author.

In private life Barbara Cartland, who is a Dame of Grace of the Order of St John of Jerusalem, Chairman of the St John Council in Hertfordshire and Deputy President of the St John Ambulance Brigade, has fought for better conditions and salaries for Midwives and Nurses.

She has championed the cause for old people, had the law altered regarding gypsies and founded the first Romany Gypsy camp in the world.

Barbara Cartland is deeply interested in Vitamin therapy, and is President of the National Association for Health.

Her designs 'Decorating with Love' are being sold all over the USA and the National Home Fashions League made her, in 1981, 'Woman of Achievement'.

Barbara Cartland's book *Getting Older, Growing Younger*, and her cookery book *The Romance of Food* have been published in Great Britain, the USA, and in other parts of the world.

THE START OF A CRUSADE

As President of the National Association for Health, I feel that I should start at the beginning and explain how I became interested in Vitamin Therapy.

When one gets old it is extraordinary how one can look back and see how things which do not seem important at the time really alter and change one's life.

My brother Ronald became a Member of Parliament for the King's Norton division in Birmingham in 1935, winning a very difficult seat in the city which had been built up by my grandfather at the end of the last Century.

Idealistic and a visionary, a young man whose principles mattered to him more than anything else, Ronald was not only the greatest influence in my life, but even now, after he was killed at Dunkirk when he was only thirty-three, people remember and talk about him.

The biography I wrote about him which had a preface by Sir Winston Churchill has just been republished with an introduction by our famous historian Sir Arthur Bryant.

Ronald was the first Tory M.P. in those days to visit the Distressed Areas where people were not only suffering through unemployment, but also the stringent restrictions of the Dole.

In Aneurin Bevan's Constituency in Wales Ronald actually saw a man dying in the street from starvation.

This shocked him so much that when he returned to London he started to fight the Government over their negligence of the Distressed Areas, and I began to work with Lady Rhys-Williams. She was giving *Vitamin B* in the form of *Marmite* to the women who were suffering from malnutrition and habitual abortion.

I was so impressed with the results, although of course what the women really needed was good food, that I began to study vitamins. I discovered that *Vitamin E,* which we now know is so important, was given in those days only to brood mares.

No one had thought that it should be taken by human beings, or that it should have such marvellous results, as I found later, in preventing miscarriages.

I also did a course on herbs at Culpeper with the famous Mrs Leyel, and I began to realise what a tremendous difference vitamins made to my life and to anyone else who took them.

After the war, when we had all been desperately short of the right food to give us the essential vitamins, I went to America, and I discovered they had the first *Vitamin B Complex* which was of course synthetic, but it did make me feel very much better. I brought some back for my children and after that became convinced that vitamins were essential.

It was not until 1955 that Rodale arrived in England and set up the Organic Vitamin Company at Hemel Hempstead, in Hertfordshire.

By that time, I was so in favour of vitamins that I wrote a book called *Vitamins for Vitality* which many people found helped them and I became more and more sure that natural vitamins, which are only PURE food, was what everybody needed.

In 1960 a brilliant man called Jimmy Lee Richardson who was the first Englishman to manufacture natural vitamins under the Healthcrafts title, suggested we should start a National Association for Health of which, as I have already said, I am the President.

It was really to give people the idea that the Health Movement was a very serious business and something to be reckoned with in the future.

I remember we had the first meeting at the Savoy and the Press kept asking:

'What is the point of it all?' and 'Isn't it quite unnecessary?'

The answer today is obvious; the Health Movement has a turnover of nearly £200 million overall, and over a quarter of everything we produce is exported, which means we are not only helping ourselves but also the economy.

It is extraordinary now, when we are all used to seeing Health Stores everywhere, and the Prince of Wales is extolling the importance of Preventive Medicine, to remember that at the time people thought we were pioneers of something quite unimportant, and laughed at me for my enthusiasm of what I knew was right.

One of the first products which captured the imagination of the public was *Biostrath*, which is full of herbs and macerated in yeast.

I heard about this herbal tonic and went to Switzerland at the invitation of Mr Pestalozzi to visit his Laboratory.

When I saw the great vats of Candida Yeast being fed with the different herbs, then the result on flowers, plants and animals, I realised this was something exceptional.

I brought it back to England, and the *Daily Mail* did the first article on it, saying it was 'something sensational'.

From that moment Biostrath sold and sold, and everybody who took it went back for more, realising how much it had helped them. Even today, with so many tonics on the market, if people are run-down and the children are nervous and under-sized, I know of nothing better than Biostrath.

I would like to tell you here the fascinating story of how, when it was first produced in Switzerland, they did a test in a school for retarded children.

There was one little girl of five or six, who sat all day drawing pictures of enormous black, frightening-looking birds. I have seen the pictures of them.

They gave her Biostrath, and gradually the birds became smaller and smaller, until at the end of two months they were changed to butterflies.

I think that story illustrates the effect that Biostrath has on small children.

It is also the only product I know which helps prevent noises in the ears, and can really improve the hearing.

People say that I 'made' Biostrath, which I suppose in a way I did, and from then I started to try everything which came onto the Health Market myself and if it worked on me, and my long-suffering family, then I recommended it.

I am proud now to be able to say that people all over the world trust me, and it is not only due to the 15,000 letters I answer a year that helps them, but that on the radio and television I am allowed to say what I think about the different products which I know are good.

I will never forget what happened when I went to speak on *Open House* to Pete Murray, who is very health-conscious.

I had taken with me for him as a present the first *Celaton CH3 Tri-Plus*, which I call more conveniently the *'Brain Pill'*, but I did not really expect him to talk about it.

Unfortunately, it was not yet in the Health Stores and when the telephonist came through to the Studio saying the lines were blocked with people asking where they could buy the 'Brain Pill', Pete Murray said to me:

'What shall I answer?'

Because I could not think of anything else, I replied:

'Oh, tell them to write to Barbara Cartland, care of "Open House".'

'You'll receive a thousand letters!' he warned.

'I can manage that!' I replied.

I had 6,000! The postmen arrived with them in sacks!

They didn't only ask about what I had spoken of to Pete Murray, but they gave me all *their* complaints, those of their husbands, their children and their mothers-in-law!

This meant there was no chance of sending them a leaflet because each one had to be answered individually. I took on two extra secretaries, and it took me two months to answer them all.

Celaton CH3 Tri-Plus, another early product, is still one of the big sellers, as people realise that it really does increase their brain capacity.

My grandsons have said that they passed their examinations on it, and quite a number of firms give it to their employees, as it improves the output of work.

I take two 'Brain Pills' every morning, and now there is something new for the brain which is called 'P.C.' (Phosphatidyl Choline). There is a very high percentage of *Lecithin* in one capsule (90 per cent) and as Linda Clark has said so often in her brilliant books in the USA: *'No Lecithin, no brain.'*

I believe the two of them combined are responsible for the twenty-five books I have written for several years running.

Another new product of which I am very proud, and

which they tell me is a best-seller, is Super G.E.B6.

G.E.B6 is a combination I thought of myself, and asked our brilliant Scientist at Healthcraft's, Dr Leonard Mervyn, to put together in the right proportions.

It contains *Ginseng,* which I learnt about first in Hong Kong in 1955, which was then comparatively unknown in this country; Vitamin E and Vitamin B6, which is the answer to all those people who think they have 'nerves', and to whom the doctors give pernicious tranquillizers and sedatives.

G.E.B6 is my reply to men who all say they will take just one or two tablets a day and no more, but it is also effective for women as well.

VITAMINS ARE NECESSARY

I thought it was very irresponsible of *Which*? Magazine to say that vitamins are unnecessary.

It seems extraordinary to me that after reports from all over the world on the decrease of vitamins in the food we eat every day due to over-use of chemicals and the pollution of the soil, sea and air that anyone should imagine that vitamins are not necessary to the human body.

Only the most bigoted people continue to say that we can get all the vitamins we require from our food. This is medically untrue. Unless one lives in the country, has free-range chickens, fresh eggs, vegetables grown with natural fertilisers like farmyard manure, it is impossible to have enough vitamins in ordinary food that one consumes daily.

There have been so many different reports on this that it seems to me strange that people have not begun to realise that the most important thing for the body, which is the most intricate machine in the world, is natural, unpolluted food which it is impossible to get without adding to our normal diet vitamins which we can take in tablet or capsule form.

It sounds crazy, but then we live in a crazy world where people deliberately pollute the sea from where we get fish, and as we know, pollute the air and soil by using chemicals which destroy the goodness nature gave us.

When I was young the top-soil on any good agricultural field in England was twelve foot. Top-soil these days often comes out of a bag and is a chemical product. This in itself is terrifying, unless one realises one can supplement the daily diet with vitamins which have been destroyed in the food by what is called 'progress'.

When one sees the side-effects of many of the so-called 'advanced medicines' one is terrified that inadvertently by taking them the results would be horrific, as reported in the case of the innumerable deaths over the 'cure' for arthritis.

What we have to remember is that the English, when they are hard-up, economise on food for the body and the brain, the first being disastrous to health.

One only has to look at the long waiting-lists in hospitals, and more especially the number of hospital beds taken up by people suffering from the side-effects of antibiotics they took for something else, to know that where it is possible to use preventive medicine it is not only more effective, but a great deal safer.

I have discovered as I have travelled in many different countries and met the scientists there that people have become much more aware than they have ever been before of the necessity for the human body to be helped and sustained with extra vitamins and minerals, some of which like *Selenium* have only recently been discovered.

It was the Americans who first realised that large doses of Vitamin E were essential to help heart disease and the Russians were one of the first to become really enthusiastic about Ginseng and *Vitamin B15*.

When I was recently in America, representing the 'Queen of Romance', I found the authors to whom I was giving awards and who had gathered together in New York for the first big Romantic Conference that had ever taken place, were far more interested in health than in love! As I pointed out to them, the two things are synonymous, and where a man and a woman are naturally healthy and feeling at their best, they will need no stimulants for love, which are now so widely available by the media.

When I think of the tremendous benefits we can attribute to the research that has been done on Vitamin B6 which, if we wish to use it, can eliminate the use of the pernicious drugs and tranquillizers with their accumulative addiction which is so dangerous, I think that anyone who says that vitamins are unnecessary cannot have studied the recent reports on the enormous benefits which have come from them which have even been reported in the *Lancet*.

All I can say is thank God for preventive medicine, whatever the critics may say. It is there for those who need it, and its tremendous advance in the last few years will not only benefit us, but our children and grandchildren in the generations to come.

IT'S ALL IN THE MIND

'It's all in the mind!' a doctor said to me when I was talking to him about the wonderful effect of vitamins on so many of my friends.

I agree with him to a certain point. Of course mankind has known from the beginning of time that if we do not have faith in ourselves, then we can achieve nothing. As I have said so often, I think a great many people retard their progress through life when they keep saying:

'It's just my luck!' 'It always happens to me!' 'I never get a break!'

I am certain these catch-phrases do not help.

Self-confidence and faith are what we should always inspire in our children and those we influence.

So many people today expect a perfect life in a perfect world for themselves. This is something we are never going to have in this dimension. Life is made up of 'ups' and 'downs'; we all experience unhappiness at some time or other.

We lose our parents through old age, our husbands and our sons through wars, and we also watch helplessly as our loved ones suffer for one reason or another.

These things are part of living, but we also have ecstatic experience of loving and being loved; of bringing children into the world; of having friendships which last through all difficulties and troubles and remain with us, even when they are over, as a beautiful memory.

What we all need, and this to me is the greatest virtue of all, is courage. It is courage that makes people believe that something better is 'round the corner', and keeps them going with the hope which is essential not only for mankind's development of what he seeks, but also for the development of himself.

What I have found, too, in a long life of helping with thousands of people, over both their health and emotional problems since the early 1930s, is that they can be helped by eating the right food.

And of course, if people believe that vitamins and a right

way of living with help them — it does.

We all know the stories of negroes in Africa who, when they have made up their minds to die, or have been told by a witch-doctor that they will do so, they die, despite the fact that there is nothing wrong with them.

It is 'mind over matter', which every doctor knows is a very strong and vital part of the human existence. Those of us who have had anything to do with hospitals are aware that people who it appears impossible to save will save themselves by sheer will-power. Others with very little wrong with them will just give up and fade away when there is really no reason for it.

That is why anyone who is a leader in any organisation or merely a strong influence in the neighbourhood in which they live must always try to inspire people with confidence in themselves and their destiny.

It is not really a very difficult thing to do, it merely means praising instead of finding fault, encouraging instead of criticising and it means saying nice things instead of passing by in an unappreciative silence.

Children particularly need encouragement when they are growing up, and are not sure of themselves or what they want, but the same applies to older people.

Many women when they get near middle-age feel afraid of losing their youth and are terrified of growing old. This is when they need the warm friendship of those around them, and the reassurance that beauty of face is not everything. It is truthfully beauty of the mind and soul which ultimately counts.

So many vitamins to-day, especially Vitamin B6, help us to have this confidence because it is a vitamin which is lacking in most of us.

Ginseng is another stimulant, not only to the body, but to the mind, and honey has, since the beginning of time, been in the words of Mohammed 'the good of the soul'.

We all of us need some form of crutch to help us through the world. We may find it in our religion, in our work, or in good health, to which all mankind is entitled in a perfect world.

It is no use thinking we are omnipotent and can manage

alone. Whatever it is that helps us on our way through life, remember it is our own faith and courage which ultimately decides whether we have helped or hindered the other people who are struggling beside us.

THE ISLE OF HONEY

A Press reporter rang me up to ask:

'Why do you think that *honey* has some magical ingredient in it?'

'Work it out for yourself,' I replied, 'the Queen Bee feeds on *Royal Jelly*. The worker bees who provide it wait on her, and she is protected by propolis with which the bees seal the comb in which she is incarcerated.

'As she never goes out, this prevents her from being attacked by any form of bacteria in the hive, and she lives for twenty years. But the wretched worker bees who roam the world live for only two months.'

So the question is: what is the magical ingredient which makes all the difference to the Queen and the honey inside the hive?

I am only stating what the Ancients believed since the beginning of time, that honey is the 'Elixir of Life'. This is the reason why honey is so important to sex and also has fantastic healing properties.

You will find this information and more in my book: *The Magic of Honey*, which has recently been republished, having been updated with all the new honey products.

The trouble is that people are so familiar with honey that they will pay pounds for a product which possesses far less minerals, vitamins and amino acids, than are present in honey.

One of the most beautiful women I ever knew in the twenties was the wife of Lord Tennyson, who Captained the English Cricket Team. Like Cleopatra, she always used honey on her face, so that she remained looking amazingly young until she was over seventy, and her skin was like that of a young child!

In those days she used to put ordinary honey on her face, but now we have many excellent honey creams which have the same effect and are not so difficult to handle.

But most of all, honey is important inside us. I am always meeting people who suffer from bronchitis, and the doctors give them all sorts of antibiotics which is most cases seem to have very little effect.

When I married my husband I was told I would be lucky if we had five years together. He had been badly wounded in the Battle of Passchendaele when a sniper's dum-dum bullet passed through his shoulder, taking away one of his lungs.

All through the twenties and into the beginning of the thirties when we were married he used to sit up all night with six pillows, coughing and finding it desperately hard to breathe.

Soon after I married him I suggested that he should take a spoonful of comb-honey in the morning and one at night.

From that moment his bronchitis practically disappeared and we had twenty-seven years of perfect happiness together until he died in 1963 when the scar-tissue from his wounds touched his heart.

Honey is such a simple remedy that people just don't have faith in it, but we have only to look back into history to realise how important it was originally.

When the Romans landed in Britain they found that beekeeping was a national industry. Everybody ate honey — of course there was no sugar in those days — with the result that the Britons were very strong and were reputed by the historians to be very beautiful.

We have only just begun to realise after all these years that honey does make people beautiful. When I see a woman with soft pink-and-white skin, the whites of her eyes clear and sparkling, her hair silky and shining, I know it is due to honey.

What is more, in these days of stress and strain, honey brings to those who eat it a calmness and serenity which also contributes to beauty.

Worry is one of the things which destroys our looks and, unfortunately, our character. It is almost impossible to worry and not be irritable and on edge. That is why honey is essential for the mother of every family, just the same as it is essential for the children.

One of the things which always annoys me in the antinatal clinics is that the mothers are told to put sugar in the bottle of water a baby drinks even when he is still breastfeeding.

It is just as easy to put in a few drops of honey, which will make the baby happy and will provide him with the many vital vitamins and minerals which are essential for a human being from the moment he comes into the world.

And remember — bed-wetting can be cured by honey as it strengthens the bladder, and elderly people who are incontinent should also take honey.

Men require honey in these tense, difficult days when finance, mortgages, employment and transport all produce their own anxieties.

If I could pass a law, I would make every man in this country take a large teaspoonful of honey, morning and night. I confidently believe that production would go up 50 per cent, exports would pour out of the country, and the Divorce Courts would be practically empty!

In fact Great Britain would have health, wealth and happiness again.

After all, we are only copying the Druids and the Pheonician traders who came to Britain in search of tin and lead who called us: 'The isle of Honey'.

Why not put back the clock?

THE WORLD'S SEARCH FOR HEALTH

AUSTRIA

Many people, like myself, have suffered during their lives with Colitis or digestive troubles that keep recurring.

It was some time before I discovered the wonders of Propolis and now, having had Diverticulitis, I take two Propolis Capsules every day of my life. They not only protect me from stomach upsets but also from the worry that I might have one!

What is Propolis?

It is one of the most effective natural medicines and was known to the Greeks, in fact the name in Ancient Greek means 'a system of defence'.

Long before the discovery of anti-biotics, of which I am always very wary, a mixture of Propolis and Vaseline was used to treat open wounds and operation cuts.

Since that time, extensive research has been carried out on Propolis, especially by the brilliant Austrian Scientist, Dr Paul Urban, and it was largely due to his encouragement and interest that Propolis was made available to the Health Movement.

In Europe, as long ago as 1969, I realised how much Health meant to the Austrians when I was asked by Dr Urban to visit Vienna.

In fact, in every country of the world there are people who are growing more and more vitally interested in Preventive Medicine.

Propolis is particularly close to my heart because it is a part of honey, which I believe is a miracle substance which we do do not fully appreciate because we are so familiar with it.

In 400 BC, Herodotus the Greek writes on the use of resin-ointments in the treatment of open wounds and abscesses, and we now know that the Greeks were aware that the bees could seal their hives against any form of disease.

It is a golden-yellow viscous substance from a tree-resin collected in particular from Poplars. The bees use this amazing substance and now, after all these years, we have discovered how we can help ourselves with it.

It is available to us all, and fantastic results have come from the very strict clinical tests which have taken place in Vienna.

In one test, 250 people were taken into hospital, all suffering from stomach ulcers, and after being treated with Propolis tincture 244 were completely healed within a fortnight.

Another test was with 59 patients with acne vulgaris, who had been suffering for several years and whose skin complaint had also withstood treatments in Dermatological University Clinics.

Within two weeks complete elimination of the acne was established, and an equal number were cured with the treatment at home.

These figures are vouched for by the specialists and doctors concerned, and there are a great number of other tests too numerous to report here, but which have all been completely successful.

I find it fascinating to think that we are now 'discovering' what the Ancients knew to be effective hundreds of thousands of years ago.

At the time of Aristotle, Propolis was used for bruises and sprains, while Pliny used it for nervous illnesses, ulcers and many other complicated conditions.

The Russians, who are always vitally interested in anything new, have found that Propolis reduces blood pressure, and they also believe it has a calming effect on the nervous system, besides using it for wounds, ulcers, skin diseases and second degree burns.

Propolis Lozenges are available to relieve throat infections, colds and influenza. They are delicious to eat and because they taste of honey children love them.

There are Propolis Capsules which should be swallowed whole for stomach upsets, or chewed for fresh breath and gum disorders.

Propolis Toothpaste will attack and prevent dental caries and there is a Skin Cream for the treatment of skin diseases.

I have recommended these products to many of the people who have written to me in despair, but who now know there is no need for them to suffer any longer.

Propolis Skin Cream is very soft and gentle to the face. It makes an ideal moisturiser of make-up base for even the most sensitive skin. It is non-allergic and contains no perfume or mineral oil.

I have given it to a number of teenagers who say it in wonderful and helps all adolescents who go through that trying time of having acne or spots, and older people find it smoothes away lines and wrinkles.

Dr Urban arranged that I should visit Vienna to receive a Civic Reception from the Mayor. I was the guest of the Austrian Society for Life Rejuvenation, and my son Ian, and Mr Maurice Hanssen, who is President of the Health Food Manufacturers Association, flew with me to Vienna Airport on a sunny day in October.

On the night we arrived, Dr Urban entertained us with a delicious dinner at the famous Sacher Hotel, and we ate Specialities, like Roe Deer cooked in cream, and of course the renowned 'Sacher Chocolate Cake'.

We visited Schonbrun Palace on Saturday in the Hofberg, which was of particular interest to me, because it had been the background for two of my books: *The Private Life of Elizabeth, Empress of Austria* and *Metternich — The Passionate Diplomat*.

It was Lord Mountbatten who told me that the Biography I wrote about the Empress, who is still adored in Austria, was considered by the Elizabethan Club to be the best that has ever been written about her.

That evening we were received by the Mayor and Lady Mayoress of Vienna in the magnificent City Hall. The Mayor, who had been in the Resistance with Dr Urban during the war, was an extremely interesting man, and he told me in his speech of welcome how, in the darkest hours of the war, he and Dr Urban were inspired and sustained by the speeches of Sir Winston Churchill.

As the Mayor's speech was in German, translated into English, and that of mine and my son's translated back into German, I was just beginning to feel tired when the doors opened and a three-piece orchestra began to play.

The Mayor rose and sang old Viennese songs by Strauss and Franz Lehar, and afterwards we danced to the strains of the 'Blue Danube'.

Before I left the Mayor told me again how much my work for health was appreciated in Austria. He also gave me a magnificent limited edition of Austrian paintings and etchings.

The last person to receive such a copy was the Queen, who had visited Vienna the previous May.

I shall always remember that marvellous and beautiful glimpse of Vienna, and I am always hoping to find time to go back.

SWEDEN

I made another interesting journey in search of health in July 1972 when John Peet of the Health and Diet Company took me to Sweden to meet the 'King of Pollen' — Gösta Carlsson, who had invented a machine for removing pollen from the fields without destroying the plants themselves.

In a delightful village in a very beautiful part of Sweden I was shown a store which contained pollen worth half a million pounds sterling.

In the same month I received a very charming letter from the King of Sweden thanking me for one of my books.

It is difficult to think of a country I have visited where the people have not wanted to talk about health.

SOUTH AMERICA

In 1972 I also visited South America. I had tasted the famous Mate Tea at REMCON, where I found it on a stand of Potters Herbal Supplies.

I was disappointed however that in Montevideo I did not see many *gauchos* with their baggy riding-breeches, huge ornamented silver spurs, cigars and wide-brimmed hats!

There, they asked me to go on television and speak, amongst other things, on health. They were at that time so old-fashioned that their camera could not move and so the performers had to walk on and off the set!

JAPAN

In Japan, where I had been in 1969, the Monks in the Temple are traditionally knowledgeable on the use of herbs.

It was at Kiyomizu, the Clear Water Temple, which was built in 759 BC, that I saw for the first time bushes, branches of trees, and even plants tied up with pieces of paper, almost as if they were curlers.

I thought at first that they were like the Tibetan and Nepalese prayer flags which fly in the wind, but the Japanese explained that they were charm papers that people received in the Temple.

If they are not the prediction required, or seem unlucky, the recipient gives them back to the Gods by tying them onto the nearest bush or tree.

What I loved more than anything in Japan were the little Buddhist Temples. I have studied Zen and I know that it is the religion of the mind.

The gardens in each Temple are plain rock set in a bed of white gravel. I told my sons that the symbolism of these gardens is that the simplicity of them stimulates the mind and suggests endless different interpretations.

After we had visited one of these Temples, a Monk gave us a special green tea which is a traditional part of Zen Buddhism.

It looked rather like green-pea soup, but it tasted delicious, and whereas before I had been feeling rather tired because we had come a long way, suddenly I felt full of vigour and energy again.

I decided after that to make better use of the health teas that can be bought at any Health Store.

TAIWAN

In Taiwan I found a treasure-trove of wonderful health products, because the Chinese are 'Medicine Men' who go right back into antiquity.

In Taipei, we all tried a Chinese massage which is famed

all over the world. My sons went for a Chinese Sulphur Bath and a massage afterwards, and I had a massage in my bedroom and I found, which I think is an excellent idea, that they teach the blind to be masseurs.

They asked me whether I wanted a man or a woman, and when I said a woman, fifteen minutes later a young girl in a white overall was led by a child into my bedroom.

If you have never had a Chinese massage, you have no idea how different it is from the European type. Their little fingers seem to find every place in your body where you have a little lump of fibrosites, calcium deposits, or anything preventing the circulation from running freely.

The Chinese may look very tiny and frail, but it was rather like being manipulated by the world's strongest man!

In the corners of the streets there were always barrows filled with fascinating herbs that had been brought in from the countryside, and as the Chinese in Taiwan are always smiling, and they seemed the happiest people one had ever seen, I cannot help feeling that their predilection for herbs may have something to do with it.

Anyway, these are some of the people who are not only keen on health today, but have known about it and lived with it for thousands of years, and it is a very wonderful experience to meet them.

WE ARE WHAT WE EAT

'WE ARE WHAT WE EAT' should be written up in every kitchen, every dining-room and every restaurant in the country. It is such an obvious truth that it is difficult for people to realise its tremendous significance.

No one would be such a fool as to put bad petrol into their car, or no petrol at all, and expect it to go, but this is just what we do to the most amazing, intricate, complex machine the world has ever known — our body!

To-day, mankind is trying to destroy itself. Farmers have poisoned the soil with aerosprays, pesticides and DDT, and the poison has seeped through the streams and rivers into the sea. Every fish caught round our shores has pesticides in it.

The Baltic Sea is so polluted that none of the fish, including the famous salmon, can be eaten, and several fishermen have died there. The romantic Mediterranean is gradually becoming a dust-bin and will, if something is not done, soon be dead like Lake Erie.

Scientists are worried because seals, who are naturally marvellous mothers, are killing their young and in a brutal and heartless way. This, they think, is due to some nerve gas which has affected their brains.

Man cannot survive without maritime life, but on top of 'dicing with death' in the sea, farmers give tranquillizers to beef cattle and to pigs so that they will fatten quicker; they caponise chickens — although in Australia it is forbidden as dangerous — with a female hormone which turns them into eunuchs; and we eat battery eggs which have no relation to the free-range variety.

On top of all that we put more than 5,000 chemicals into our food. These chemicals thicken, thin, colour, flavour, etc., but none has any nutritive value. They also kill the vitamins by which we live!

Are you then surprised that in this over-chemicalised world we have, to be really well, to put back into our bodies what ought to be on our plates — i.e. the natural vitamins these chemicals destroy?

People who say we get all the vitamins we need in our

food have not looked at our over-crowded hospitals, with a waiting-list of over half a million; they have not waited nine to thirteen weeks to see a Consultant, or sometimes ten years for an operation!

Subsidiary diseases each account for the loss of millions of working hours per year. The number of colds and influenza sufferers runs into such astronomical figures that one can scarcely believe them.

And yet how do people eat?

It has been estimated that 25 per cent of the British population do not have breakfast, and another 50 per cent do not eat the right foods containing vitamins and minerals. Every doctor has scores of people daily surging into his surgery telling him they are 'run down', and want a tonic.

'If every one of my patients ate a proper breakfast of bacon and eggs, a spoonful of honey, *Bran*, a small pot of *yoghurt* and an unsprayed apple,' a well-known physician told me, 'I would be able to put my feet up for a change!'

A recent industrial survey showed that men and women are at their physical and mental best an hour after a meal. Yet how many illnesses are acquired because a commuter gets into a crowded train with an empty stomach?

What is more, to go without breakfast means that you are cheating yourself and your employer.

'We are crazy,' a dietician said to me. 'We study to pass examinations in chemistry, physiology, teaching, electronics and so on, but no one really bothers to study how the men and women who do all these things should eat to get the best out of their brains and their bodies.'

'Nerves' are one of the most talked-about diseases of the century. One woman in nine has a nervous breakdown. 'It's my nerves,' a woman will tell you, having no idea she is really suffering from a form of malnutrition.

When I was young we were told not to think about ourselves. To-day I beg people to study themselves.

At a meaning of the Royal Society for Health an eminent doctor said: 'By the age of forty a man is either a fool or his own physician.'

We can be healthy, we can combat disease, we can keep young, all by eating the right foods. What is more, food affects our characters, our personalities and, of course, our happiness.

I have often said that if a farmer fed his animals as badly as the average housewife feeds her husband, the RSPCA would sue him!

'That isn't fair!' a housewife wrote to me after I had said this on the air.

'What do you give him?' I asked when I replied to her letter.

'He has a cereal breakfast because he goes out so early,' she answered, 'and he has to have a sandwich lunch at work; but I give him something tasty at night. I admit it's usually out of a tin, but I cook it carefully, and he has instant potatoes and frozen peas — so he gets his green vegetables.'

Can you see how little protein that man was getting?

A man, to be strong, healthy and a good lover needs eighty grams a day. The average helping of roast beef is seventeen grams!

I believe one of the most important ways to be healthy is to keep your eating to a time-table. I know so many men who rush off to the office with only a cup of coffee, have a sandwich lunch any time between twelve o'clock and two, then go seven or eight hours before eating dinner or supper. These are the men who have duodenal ulcers and heart-attacks!

'How can I feed my family the right way?' I am asked over and over again by the ordinary housewife.

I admit it's difficult, but you can buy as much as possible from Health Stores. They are your best and truest friends. If you live in the country you can get free-range chickens from a farm, in London you go to Marks and Spencers. Their chickens grow up in the green pasture land of Worcestershire, they go into the shops untouched and unfrozen, and those that are not sold are never kept until the following day.

Bread made from stone ground (compost-grown) wheat tastes very different from the ordinary, lifeless white variety. Vegetables which have been rattled to Covent Garden from Bedfordshire and back again to the local shops haven't much Vitamin C in them. Try to grow a few yourself, even if it's in a window-box, or only mustard and cress on a flannel.

The answer is quite simple — we must choose foods which are not poisoned with chemicals, preservatives and white sugar, and we must supplement our ordinary meals with the magical, wonderful vitamins, which can bring us radiant, glowing good health.

Vitamins have become a controversial subject, yet all over the world people are beginning to realise how tremendously important they are to life.

In West Germany to-day there are 3,000 Health Stores, and every small market-place has what they call a 'Biological stall', which means the vegetables and fruit have been grown on land where pesticides, aerosprays and DDT have not been used.

In Britain, we have not yet reached a thousand Health Stores, but every day we have more and more demands from people all over the country saying how important they feel a Health Store is to their well-being.

But people do not know what to order, and many live miles away from a Health Store, so to help them there is the Health and Happiness Club, which will not only post them what they need, but explain the importance of each product.

What is so disturbing to those who are trying to eat right and keep well are the scientists and doctors who state categorically in the press or on the air that vitamins are unnecessary, or that we can eat too many. The trouble is that these people have never studied natural vitamins and they cannot see the enormous difference which exists between synthetic and natural vitamins.

Synthetic vitamins are made from chemicals, and when we are taking them, we are only putting another chemical into our already over-chemicalised bodies.

Here is a story which explains the difference very clearly. My doctor was a prisoner-of-war in Singapore, and when the Japanese were beaten and the Allies flew in, they brought for the thousands of starved and ill prisoners food, and a certain amount of vitamins. In those days vitamins were, of course, synthetic because natural ones had not yet been discovered.

The majority of the men in prison cams were suffering from beri-beri, which is a lack of Vitamin B. A handful of polished rice per day was all they had been given for the exhausting, brutal labour they had been forced to do by their captors.

In the camp where my doctor had been interned the majority of prisoners were, after a few days of being given food and vitamins, well enough to be flown to hospital. But there were thirty-six men left who were on the point of death.

The doctors, and there were quite a number of them there, naturally wanted to go home themselves, but they could not leave the men who were so ill in the care of the Japanese who had behaved with such ghastly brutality over the four years of war. So they consulted together and asked the Japanese if they would bring them some rice polishings.

Rice polishings are the outer husks of rice, which are thrown away, and which are pure, natural Vitamin B; while people eat the inner kernel which has no goodness in it whatsoever.

The Japanese, only too willing to do anything now that they were conquered, brought the rice polishings, and the doctors made a concoction from it which smelt terrible and tasted worse — but it was natural Vitamin B. Then the doctors said to these thirty-six men who were dying:

'You have to drink six pints of this a day.'

Now here is the miracle — and it is set down in all the medical histories of the time — within twenty-four hours, every single one of those men was well enough to be flown to hospital. They were still desperately ill, but they were not so ill that they could not be moved.

That is the difference between synthetic vitamins and natural vitamins. While synthetic vitamins may help some people, a natural vitamin is always helpful — and I have never yet known a side-effect of any sort from somebody taking natural vitamins.

Natural vitamins are food and experiments are going on all the time, but we do know that vitamins work as a team, and it is wisest for someone who wants to enrich their diet with food supplements to take a natural multi-vitamin tablet from a Health Store.

Once you have the foundation of a multi-vitamin tablet like Gev-E-Tabs, then you can begin to see after a few weeks what else is wrong.

If you have weak eyes, those that feel gritty, or which respond badly to bright lights, then you need *Vitamin A* and *Vitamin B2*.

If you suffer from bad circulation, heart trouble, varicose veins or nerves, then you need *Vitamin E*.

There is a natural vitamin to relieve or cure every type of ill health, but it is important that *natural* vitamins should be taken in conjunction with multi-vitamin tablets, which supply all the vitamins the average person needs every day, and all the minerals as well.

I am continually astounded at how quickly vitamins, if they are the right ones, can work.

A short time ago a very important police officer from Hong Kong came to see me. He arrived at my house for lunch on Sunday with a very bloodshot eye and a huge swelling beneath it. Thinking perhaps he had been in one of the riots which were then very prevalent in the East, I asked him what had occurred.

'I really don't know,' he repled, 'I've had this bad eye for three months. I've seen various doctors but none of them can find out what is wrong. I'm hoping to find time to go to Moorfields Eye Hospital while I'm in England.'

I gave him a packet of multi-vitamin tablets and some Vitamin B2 capsules from my store cupboard. I told him to take two of the multi-vitamin tablets every day, and four of the natural B2. On Monday evening he telephoned me and said:

'You won't believe it, but the bloodshot effect in my eye has almost gone, and I'm quite certain the swelling is going down too!'

By Thursday he was completely cured! What he was suffering from was a vitamin deficiency, and yet none of the doctors he had seen had any idea that this was the cause of his bad eye.

So let me say again that when something goes wrong with our health, we need the right food rather than medicine, and natural vitamins *are* food.

WE BECOME WHAT WE THINK

It is known that by the time we reach middle-age our character is written on our face! That means our innermost feelings are gradually visible to the world. In other words, '*we become what we think*'.

I have always been convinced that a woman can make her children beautiful if, while she is pregnant, she thinks only beautiful thoughts.

When my daughter and sons were on the way I never read unpleasant books, or watched horror films and I tried to 'think' them beautiful and clever.

I succeeded in that my daughter was acclaimed the most beautiful girl in England and my two sons are handsome, charming, considerate and very loving.

What I believe is important is not only to read books which inspire one, but also to look at pictures which elevate the mind and make one 'feel' beauty as well as see it.

One artist who did this so perfectly was Francis Marshall. For thirty years he illustrated my novels. I know how much I owe to him my success in being the most prolific author in the world, and to have sold 370 million books.

In my novels I write about love which is both physical and mental and which comes from the Divine. Francis translated what I was trying to say into the faces of the beautiful and alluring heroines who have made women of every nation wish to emulate them.

He gave the women he drew the eyes of a pure and innocent girl whose heart pulsated with love and to whom God and everything that was good were part of her whole being.

That is every woman's ideal, what she longs to be, even if she fails herself and those who believe in her.

Francis was a sensitive and very perceptive man and these qualities show in his drawings and made him able to illustrate the people I described exactly as I imagined them.

It was a great gift, and everybody who sees the lovely pictures he gave me to hang on the walls in my home feels that he uplifts their hearts and, I believe, their souls so that they become better and finer people.

I miss Francis Marshall desperately and in this age of pornography, vulgarity and violence the world will miss him too.

There are few enough people left to help us 'think' ourselves as we wish to be, so that it shows in our faces, like a light in the darkness.

THE MILK OF HUMAN KINDNESS

When I first came to Camfield Place in 1950, I supervised a farm of 500 acres. We had a milking herd and 52 Wessex Saddleback Pigs. I had always been interested in vitamins and I thought that if human beings wanted them so did animals.

I thought the cheapest and best method of giving vitamins to my pigs would be *Brewers' Yeast*, which I obtained from a local Brewery. In those days I could buy a whole tubful of yeast for ten shillings! I gave this to my farrowing sows and also my boars and for several years had a record number of litters for the country and, I think, the whole country.

The first year we had an average of twelve piglets out of fifty-two sows and it only gradually went down over the years as the sows became older.

Later, when I was speaking three times a week on vitamins, I would tell my audiences of women about Brewers' Yeast and what a difference it makes to one's life.

'It's the milk of human kindness,' I said. 'If you nag your husband, slap your children and hate your neighbours you are short of Vitamin B. The easiest way to take it is Brewers' Yeast tablets. But one word of warning: I gave Brewers' Yeast to my sows and they all had abnormally large litters!'

There would be a moment of stupefied silence — then, as they got the point, a roar of laughter!

Since then there has been a great deal of research done on Vitamin B, and a great many divisions of the main vitamin. Although the chemical structure of each of the B vitamins is quite different, they act co-ordinately on the different enzyme systems of the body. They also do not store for very long, and diets containing too little of the B vitamins can lead to multiple deficiency diseases within a few months.

What I think the scientists have proved is that the B Group of vitamins should be regarded as a complex, that all members are essential and, to a great extent, inter-dependent upon each other. This is important because we have all begun to realise that many of the derivatives are essential to us personally.

For instance, I find that my eyes need Vitamin B2 and nearly everybody who writes to me with health problems needs Vitamin B6. This is particularly important for older people as a lack of B6 can give rise to depression and mental confusion, or to put it in a more common phrase — 'nerves'.

I believe to be really well we need all the B vitamins and that is why I am delighted with the new high potency B-Complex formula: *'Hi-Comp-B 50'* from American Nutrition. It contains every B vitamin in a large, but balanced quantity in each tablet. One tablet should be enough for the ordinary person, but again it is essential that you check what you personally need. Everyone, as I have said so often, is different, and I find, for instance, that I can take only the very smallest amount of Nicotinamide.

B2 is marvellous for people who have anything wrong with their eyes, a loss of hair, a malfunction of the liver or, which is more prevalent than one thinks, an itching skin. Here again, I find that even if you are taking extra amounts of B2 it is wise to take B-Complex as well.

Doctors have said that women during pregnancy of taking a contraceptive pill should increase the Vitamin B6 they take and apart from this, a lack of B6 can give one dermatitis, an inflamed mouth and tongue, and cracked lips.

I always advise anyone who is taking antibiotics from the doctor to take at the same time large amounts of Vitamin B, which will prevent side-effects. If you ever have a late night in which you have eaten and drunk far more than you normally do, take a *Hi Comp-B50* before you go to bed, and you will be amazed at how well you feel in the morning.

To return to my first love, Brewers' Yeast, I still think that this is one of the most complete and natural forms of the B vitamins, as well as the cheapest.

Besides containing most of the B-Complex, there are also seventeen amino acids, fourteen minerals, and it is practically free from fat and carbohydrates.

For Old Age Pensioners, who can afford to buy only one

vitamin I always recommend Brewers' Yeast, and I have seen what appears to be miraculous results on their health, especially amongst those who are not eating the right food because they cannot afford enough protein.

Anyway, I am convinced that everybody needs Vitamin B, in whatever form you take it, in order to keep well.

It will also help you to be sweet, good-tempered and avoid family squabbles, which always make everybody concerned miserable.

MY SEARCH FOR HEALTH GOES ON

'Why are you so interested in herbs?'

This is a question I am asked over and over again, on the radio, on television, in the letters from people who write to me about their health and, of course, by my friends, and behind this question lurks an even more important one:

'How do you know so much?'

Perhaps people today are so impressed by those who have letters after their names or diplomas on the wall that they are slightly suspicious of those who can't produce such official documentation of their knowledge.

The story of my interest in herbs began when I was a child at the beginning of the century. My parents lived in Worcestershire in the Vale of Evesham, and my earliest recollection was of the garden and the land around us filled with trees covered in pink and white blossom, giving a fairy-tale beauty to the landscape.

Later there would be plums, huge golden ones, known as 'Pershore Plums', and the deep red ones which hung from the trees like the fruit in some mythical legend.

Hidden behind all this beauty however there was great poverty and streets where children ran barefoot, and often in rags, playing in the gutters; dark alleys where policemen would not venture on a Saturday night; and small cottages scattered over the countryside where there were old people living on a mere sustenance, and who were ill, but unable to pay a doctor to attend them.

Two or three times every week I would go with my mother or Nanny to call on these cottagers, taking soup or jelly, which my mother believed would help those who were afflicted.

All down the years I can hear the old countryfolk talking of dandelion tea, which they took for their liver, of parsley, which they believed, quite rightly, would ease disturbances in the bladder and kidneys, and rhubarb, which they all believed was the right laxative.

In season they would speak of other things. I remember my Nurse telling an old woman that I had an 'upset tummy'.

'What Miss Barbara needs is blackberry juice,' she said.

It was many years before I was to realise how good this advice was, for the astringent and tonic properties of the English wild blackberry are excellent for the summer diarrhoea of children, and inflammation of the intestinal tract.

Cowslip was another flower which was discussed, although it was sometimes called 'Palsywort'. In those days I didn't understood why they whispered about it in low voices, but later I learnt that the cowslip had a reputation for curing tumours of the uterus.

Parsley was what the old countryfolk swore by for the bladder and the kidneys.

'Oi'll make meself a pot o' parsley tea,' I remember a very old man saying when my mother asked if there was anything she could bring him to help the excruciating pain he was suffering with a stone.

All these things remained in my mind as I grew up, and my mother believed in such natural remedies as hot blackcurrant tea when I had a cold, and honey and glycerine if I had a cough.

But it wasn't until the beginning of the thirties that I met Mrs Leyel of Culpeper, perhaps the most famous herbal practitioner of the century.

I went to see her because I was suffering from a form of colitis owing to having passed through a time of deep unhappiness, which had affected me both mentally and physically, until my whole digestive system was upset.

Mrs Leyel was an entrancing person. One had only to speak to her to be enthused by her love of healing, by the aura of kindness she emitted to all who consulted her, by the fund of knowledge that seemed to bubble out of her with every sentence she spoke.

'Of course I can help you,' she said, and from those simple words there began my close friendship with this woman who was much older than I was, but who seemed to me to speak a language of commonsense, and to endow it with a strange magic which attracted me as nothing had ever done before.

Mrs Leyel opened my eyes to the whole possibility of

healing. For two years I saw her regularly, and she told me of the cures she had made, of the diseases she was treating, and of the amazing success she had had by persuading people not to take doctors' medicines, but to go back to Nature.

'Nature has given us the cure for every disease,' she said, 'although we do not realise it.'

It was Mrs Leyel who first talked to me of the danger of synthetic medicines. She was convinced that in the years to come, drugs made by chemists would prove to be destructive, and the side-effects unpredictable. How right she was!

But hers was a small, quiet voice speaking in the wilderness, and no one heeded her warning.

It is impossible for me to describe all I learnt from Mrs Leyel. Today her books are always near me when I write, and what delight I find in reading them over and over again; enthralled not only by their message of healing, but also by the fantastic amound of research she did. And who would not enjoy her unquenchable sense of humour?

I was still studying with Mrs Leyel when I went to Baden-Baden with a friend to stay at Dr Dengler's Sanatorium, which was then famous. Dr Dengler was a courtly, remarkable man with an almost clairvoyant power of diagnosis.

He had evolved a treatment, not only for people who lived too luxuriously, and had become fat and soft in the process, but also for those who were suffering from complaints of the intestines and deterioration of the liver, especially those who had lived in hot climates.

His Sanatorium was fashionable; at the same time, out of the kindness of his heart, he had a great many patients who paid him very little, if anyting at all.

Dr Dengler and I became close friends. For three years I went back, not only as a patient, but as a student, to learn from him about his work and to discover how exciting and unusual his findings were.

He was the first man ever to use unsaturated fat as an internal cure for colitis and diseases of the liver. Deep irrigations were given with olive oil, and the results were fantastic.

There was a funny sight to be seen when staying in Dr Dengler's Sanatorium. All the patients were woken very early in the morning when we were obliged to take a rather nasty dose of salts — some special concoction of the doctor's. We then dressed and were told to walk to the top of the mountain just outside the Sanatorium.

It was a lovely walk through the pinewoods and, when the sun was shining and the flowers vivid over the countryside, it could be an hour of absolute delight. But almost at the moment when we reached the top the salts began to work and we would all hurry back to the Sanatorium at double-quick time!

I remember racing past Dr Buchman of the Oxford Movement; Lady Ludlow, one of the richest women in England, and the Viscount Castlerosse, who weighed over twenty stone and was the great wit of the period: all of us intent on one thing only — to reach the Sanatorium!

Dr Dengler was the first man to advocate a slimming cure where people were given protein, rather than told to eat practically nothing. It was just becoming fashionable to slim and many places insisted on a great deal of fruit-juice and very little else.

Dr Dengler gave his patients plenty of meat, not much fruit, no bread, no starch, but well-balanced meals spaced out over the day.

He was ahead of his time, and I believe we have now come back to realising that what is so important in combating obesity is that people should not starve themselves, but eat small meals regularly, meals that are principally based on protein.

One year in August, I stayed at a fascinating Spa at Aix-les-Bain. This was high up in the mountains, and always there was the sound of rushing water falling in torrents down the mountainside into the lakes below.

It was Sir Louis Knutsen, Physician in Ordinary to the Princess Royal, who told me that the sound of flowing water is soothing to the brain.

Water calms the mind and takes away strain and tension, and that is why so many politicians and doctors choose a fishing holiday as a means of relaxation.

It was at Aix-les-Bain that I experienced for the first time massage under water.

REJUVENATION

At the end of the thirties I met a very remarkable man. He was a French doctor who had been experimenting in France on rejuvenation and keeping people young and active. His research had shown him that a person needs their hormones to be balanced. He therefore often gave women masculine hormones and vice versa. I worked with him, seeing his experiments, discussing many new products and finding his theories absolutely fascinating, right up to the outbreak of war.

He was then the first man I know in England to give vitamin injections. He gave the injection in the vein of large doses of Vitamin B and Vitamin C. He cured a friend of mine of acute and agonising sciatica, and with his hormone injections I saw him keep both men and woman young and active, long after their contemporaries had begun to crumble into old age.

He was always trying out new things. Being a very brilliant doctor he could practise in France, in America, in Switzerland, and in England. He was the first person I knew to bring Dr Nieheim's method of cell therapy to England.

He was also almost the first person I was in touch with who believed, like the Americans, in 'pre-hospitalisation' treatment, so that the patient was 'fighting fit' before he or she had an operation, rather than being treated after it was over.

I can't tell you how exciting it was learning from this friend of mine, seeing the often marvellous results from his theories. We kept intouch all through the war, but when it was over he went to live in Switzerland. From there he sent me reports ofwhat he was doing until about five years ago when he died.

During the war I was living in Bedfordshire, where I was Services Welfare Officer to about 15 thousand of the armed services. I was also, after 1942, an officer in the St John Ambulance Brigade. I became the County Cadet officer and, having recruited over two thousand cadets, I found I had no officers to train them.

It was therefore essential that I should have officers very quickly, but in those days an officer had to have six lectures from a doctor before they could be appointed. English doctors were up to their eyes in work, but the Americans, pouring into Great Britain with their Flying Fortresses came to my rescue.

In my house at Great Barford, two or three times a week, there were lectures given by American doctors in first-aid. Of course, when these were over we would sit and talk on all sorts of medical matters. It gave me an interesting insight into the new developments in places all over America. There were doctors from Texas, from Virginia, from Ohio and Maryland, all of them having different ideas on medical surgery and physiology matters.

When I first visited America in 1946 it was however my first real introduction to vitamins. My American friends said to me with glee:

'We have found something wonderful! We've discovered a capsule which, if you take it after drinking, you don't feel any after-effects the following morning. It's amazing!'

It was a capsule of *Vitamin B Complex*, synthetic because all vitamins were synthetic in those days. I tried it, not because I was drinking very much, but I realised how depleted of vital nutrients we were during the war through shortage of food, and the tremendous unhappiness and anxiety we had passed through.

I took the Vitamin B capsule back to England. It was very expensive, but I managed to get the product sent to me regularly for the next few years. I gave it to my husband, myself and my children.

Because I was so enthusiastic about it, more and more people became interested. In fact, friends coming from America began bringing me different vitamin products which had been produced there. It was later that a factory was set up by an American firm in Hemel Hempstead. They produced the first natural vitamins in Great Britain.

Before this however I had nearly died. I had a very bad hysterectomy. I was on the operating table for a very long time. I lost a great deal of blood and was, I believe, not properly treated afterwards. Certainly no 'pre-hospitalisation' was done for me before the operation!

I was quite convinced I was dying and I insisted that my husband brought me home in an ambulance.

'I must get home,' I told him, 'and I'll change my doctors. I'm too ill now to argue, or to insist on seeing other specialists, please, let us go home, then I can start again.'

He did as I wished, and I asked the local doctor, whom I had met only once before, to come and see me. I had meant to ask for several senior specialists to come from London, but there was no need.

My local doctor had been a prisoner in Singapore. He had seen the terrible effects of beri-beri on men who had worked on the Burma road. Beri-beri is, of course, a lack of Vitamin B.

He came every day and gave me vitamin injections and vitamins to take. They were synthetic because natural vitamins were not then obtainable, but even with those I felt myself getting better day by day. I was operated on at the beginning of October, and, although I was very shaky, I wrote a book before Christmas.

It was then I swore to myself that I would learn everything there was to learn about natural medicine, natural vitamins and a natural way of health. It is something I have done conscientiously ever since.

I am close friends with people like Professor Ana Aslan in Romania, who invented the H3. I have friends in Europe and America who send me the results of their clinical trials, who tell me of every new experiment and invention which seems likely to be of benefit to mankind.

I have many friends, too, among the dieticians in America, in fact, one of the most exciting moments for me was when I discovered *Look Younger, Live Longer* by Gayelord Hauser. When I met him some years ago I said to him:

'Your book was an inspiration to me. I told me all I had believed in, but at the time had never been able to put into words.'

Today, through the National Association for Health, I am in touch with many different people, and in my travels I have met the Minister concerned with Health in the particular country I am visiting. He has always put me in touch with the appropriate Scientists and Professors concerned with herbs and natural products. In Mexico and Japan, particularly, I had most enlightening and constructive discussions with many authorities.

There have been many things with which I have experimented and learnt during the years: I have seen diagnoses made under trance; I have seen the results of an operation performed by the laying on of healing hands; I have seen miraculous and unbelievable cures for stones in the bladder, and growths in the chest and in the throat, performed by 'Absent Healing'.

I have also seen, and know, that faith will cure where all else has failed and there is no other hope left.

I have studied Yoga and met Yogis, and those who believe that right breathing is the basis of health. I have talked with a man in India who was over 126 years old. I have seen people who looked as young at ninety as when they were thirty.

I am certain we are at the beginning of a new understanding, and enlightenment.

Mankind, while doing his best to destroy himself by chemicals, pesticides and drugs, is yet aware instinctively that Nature can still save him and those he loves, if he will just have the good sense to give Nature a chance!

PROTEIN IS THE PASSPORT TO HEALTH

We have thirty billion cells in our bodies, and they are all made of protein. So are our arteries, colon, glands, muscles, skin, bones, teeth, eyes, and hair.

More than one twelfth of the body cells die and are replaced every day. The cell replacement *must be protein*.

No one would be so stupid as to try to mend a rubber motor-tyre with paste and water, but that is exactly what we do when we try to keep our cells alive and recreate others with starch, sugar, and every sort of carbohydrate!

'What exactly is protein?' I am asked at every meeting.

'Meat, chicken, game, fish, eggs and cheese are the easiest methods of taking protein,' I reply, 'and do start at breakfast.'

'I don't feel like eating in the morning,' many people say.

'What do you have for breakfast?' I ask.

'I usually just grab a cup of coffee before rushing to the office!'

After a fast of nearly twelve hours one's metabolism, or blood sugar (no relation to ordinary sugar), is down to 80 to 120 milligrams in about 100 cc of blood.

If you start rushing about, the blood sugar falls to 70 milligrams. You are hungry and you have less energy, so you become agitated, irritated and depressed.

We all know the person who says:

'I feel ghastly in the morning. I have to be dragged out of bed! I really don't get going until the afternoon.'

Now what puts up the blood sugar to the average 90 to 95 milligrams which it should be?

PROTEIN!

In one study on blood sugar, 200 volunteers ate different types of breakfast.

After black coffee alone, the blood sugar dropped and the volunteer experienced irritability, hunger, fatigue, exhaustion and headaches, with all the symptoms getting worse as the morning progressed.

Two pieces of toast, coffee with sugar and milk caused a quick rise and within an hour a quick fall!

Two eggs (protein), wholemeal bread (or, better still, bran) and honey produced a high level which was maintained all through the morning.

Are you surprised that I say people who do not eat a proper protein breakfast are cheating themselves, and their employers?

Some more facts: Cancer, tooth decay, diabetes, arthritis and a dozen other degenerative diseases are unknown among the primitive Eskimos. Explorers have told us that the Eskimos are a very happy race. They laugh a great deal and have incredible powers of endurance.

'What do Eskimos eat?' is the obvious question.

The answer is reindeer meat, salmon — usually raw, and other fish. All unspoilt, unchemicalised protein. There is an obvious lesson here, and an American research Professor has written:

'Protein from animal sources provide a suitable selection of amino acids for building human tissue. Plant sources are considerably less efficient.'

This particular report goes on to say:

'Animal proteins have the highest co-efficient of digestibility, rating 95 to 100 per cent.'

This is the reason why I am so keen that people should realise how essential protein is to health, youth and beauty.

Dogs and cats are often fed far better than children. As a result, many children suffer from *poproteinosis*, a deficiency disease caused by insufficient protein in their daily diet.

Parents often complain that their children will not eat a protein meal at mealtimes, but if you enquire into what the child eats in between times you will find he drinks a lot of milk, gobbles ice-cream, potato crisps, chocolate, and other sweets whenever he can get them.

This means he is not hungry for the body-building foods he should be having at least three times a day.

'Even a quart of milk a day will not provide sufficient nourishment for proper growth and development,' a doctor told me, 'and it is often this consumption of milk which impairs the child's appetite for solid foods.'

If protein is essential to children, how tremendously important it is to an adult suffering from the strain and stress of modern living!

I am convinced that practically every disease, including cancer, can be the result of wrong feeding, and I can quote many clinical experiments to support this contention.

I suppose the first time I realised how important protein is for strength and energy was when the Olympic Games were held in Great Britain, after the war. I was told that the Russian competitors had brought their own food with them.

'What do they eat?' I asked.

'Steak and honey,' was the answer.

As they did phenomenally well, it was obvious that diet was all-important.

Since then, having studied the subject very thoroughly, I am convinced that the day will come when employers in industry will realise that if they give their employees a proper protein breakfast as soon as they arrive for work, the increase in production will more than justify the cost.

Women in general eat less protein food than men, and anaemia is therefore more common to them. It was announced recently that one woman in two is anaemic. This condition is quickly corrected when the protein intake is increased and Vitamin B12 is taken.

There is also an organic iron tonic which has no side-effects. Ordinary iron has always been a difficult thing to absorb, and often entails constipation, headaches and various other troubles.

'*Florodix*' has made an amazing difference to the lives of thousands and thousands of women both in Great Britain and on the Continent.

So many people write to me complaining of indigestion. When protein is inadequate the digestive enzymes are insufficiently produced.

What is more, the tiny muscles surrounding the intestinal tract become weak and stringy, like old rubber bands. This means the movement of the intestinal tract cannot work properly and undigested food causes flatulence and pain.

'A man whose bowels move regularly and normally will live very long.'

That is as true today as when Herodicus of Sezymdria wrote it thousands of years before Christ.

One evidence of protein deficiency that women often ignore is that finger-nails split, break off and fail to grow. Doctors have even used the rate of nail growth to measure protein adequacy.

What is not generally known is that many drugs stop one's nails growing, and the degree to which the nails are affected indicates the toxicity of the drug.

'My nails look terrible!' a friend said to me when she came out of hospital. 'What can I do about them?'

'Eat a beef-steak every day,' I answered.

She was astonished, but she took my advice, and by adding 2 Super Gev-E-Tabs (multi-vitamin tablets), 4 Dolomite tablets and 100 mg of Vitamin A Compleat to her diet, she was soon delighted with her long, elegant finger-nails.

It is often difficult to eat the right food after an operation, a burn or an accident, especially where children are concerned, because of nausea and lack of appetite. Yet those who know the principles of emergency feeding, which is based on protein and honey, are usually thrilled by the rapid healing, and sometimes quite spectacular recovery.

I often think of a wise old schoolmaster who told me:

'If I have bad news for one of my pupils, I keep it to myself until after the boy has had a meal. Even tragedy can be endured more easily on a full stomach.'

Doctors have estimated that as much as 80 to 100 grams of complete protein should be consumed daily to build up a good resistance to infection and to ensure that, physically and mentally, one is at the top of one's form.

It has also been said very often that a man, to be a good lover, needs 80 grams of protein a day.

(See my table on page 58.)

I appreciate that protein-giving foods are expensive, but if one eliminates or drastically reduces the unessential foods, then you will find the cost almost levels itself out.

And remember, while the French spend half their weekly wage on food, the British economise on the one thing they shouldn't — the maintenance of their health and strength.

Yet whatever food you eat, you also need extra vitamin supplements, and these can help enormously to build up one's intake of protein.

In one excellent product, the 'Brain Pill', which I find amazingly rejuvenating, the protein content of even one tablet is very high, so one doesn't have to rely entirely on the kitchen.

These tablets are bought in their thousands every week by the proprietor of a manufacturing company for his workers. Production, he says, has risen by 25 per cent since they started to take them.

I am sure that not only every part of our body needs protein, but so does the brain. That is why I have been thrilled by the 'Brain Pill' (Celaton CH3 Tri-Plus), which feeds the brain.

I have achieved the world record for seven years by writing — in this order — 21, 24, 20, 23, 24, 24 and 25 books.

This was possible after years of writing an average of six books a year because I took two tablets of the Brain Pill in the morning, which contain a large amount of protein, and two Ginseng tablets, which again have a great deal of protein in them.

It is very important for people who must have a surgical operation to have enough protein. Undernourished and ill individuals are poor suicidal risks, have adverse reactions to anaesthetics, are susceptible to shock, and heal slowly.

Animals deficient in protein for only five days prior to an operation take twice as long to heal, even though they are given adequate protein afterwards.

For those who are dedicated to Vegetarianism, there is Soya Flour, which is very easy to obtain these days. Soya Flour, as you see on my table below, is very high in protein — higher than steak.

But you must study it! It is no use saying: 'I'm Vegetarian,' and just giving up meat.

I had a letter from a man of twenty-seven recently who said he and his wife of the same age couldn't make love. I found they had both suddenly become Vegetarians, and were living on nothing but carbohydrates.

People in famine areas and in Concentration Camps have always reported loss of sexual interest. Autopsy studies of poorly nourished men and women of a sexually active age have shown shrivelled ovaries and testicles.

Women who slim the wrong way — decreasing instead of increasing their protein intake — and men suffering from stress who do not eat enough protein containing Vitamins B6 and E can destroy their sex urge completely.

Be a Vegetarian, but do take care of that exciting, complicated, intricate and very wonderful machine you call your body! That is a message to us all. No one yet has invented anything so marvellous as the body!

A GUIDE TO THE MORE USUAL SOURCES OF PROTEIN

PROTEIN	AMOUNT	GRAMS OF PROTEIN
STEAK	AVERAGE HELPING	21
BEEF	"	17
LAMB	"	15
CHICKEN	"	18
LIVER	"	19
SALMON	"	22
YOGHOURT	ONE QUART	33
CHEESE	ONE PIECE (2OZ)	12
SOYA FLOUR	ONE CUP	37

ARTHRITIS

In the past few years arthritis and rheumatism have increased dramatically without there being any really effective products with which to cure or even relieve the misery and distress it brings to so many people.

Human beings and animals have suffered from arthritis since the beginning of time. In fact some years ago, when they were widening a road on part of my husband's land in Scotland the bulldozer unearthed the grave of a chieftain's daughter who had been buried in pre-Viking days.

Although she had been quite young when she died, the doctors found signs of arthritis on the bones of her skeleton.

I started what has been a terrible saga of pain and discomfort in February 1974, when I fell down in front of the Taj Mahal — by moonlight! Everybody laughs when I tell them this, but from my point of view it was a disaster!

The gateway to the Taj Mahal has a very high step and the Indians, instead of shining their torches on our feet, shone them on our faces. I caught my toe on the step and fell forward making my leg bleed very badly.

What I did not realise at the time was that I had put out the base of my spine. This pressed on the sciatic nerve and within a month I was in agony.

I then started the long trek of trying to find someone to help me.

I went to six osteopaths and had traction, I had acupuncture, I had injections! I took dozens of different so-called 'cures' for rheumatism, arthritis, sciatica and gout!

Nothing really helped and the only suggestion I had from doctors was that I should have the surgical operation which meant cutting off the end of the spine. This I was determined not to do!

I was becoming desperate. I had reached the stage where I couldn't walk for more than a few yards, and it was very painful to turn over in bed. In fact I had to pull my legs round with both hands.

Then a friend told me that she had seen on a television programme an amazing man called MacManaway talking to Ludovic Kennedy. It was said that he could do marvels with bad backs.

Because I had nothing to lose, I wrote to Major MacManaway, care of the BBC, and asked if he ever came to London, as I understood he lived in Scotland.

He rang up and gave me an appointment, and I actually had no idea he was a Healer, until I arrived at his mother's flat and met the most charming and delightful old lady of eighty, who told me she had been a Healer for thirty years.

'I worked very hard, but I never took money for what I did to help people,' she told me. 'But my son has a wife and three children, and as he has left the army to continue his work, he therefore has to charge a small fee.'

It was in fact a very small fee, but as soon as I met Major MacManaway I felt that he had very special powers. I learnt later that he had discovered his power of healing in 1940 and later with his wife founded the Westlake Healing and Touching Centre in Scotland.

To my great relief I did not have to undress, I merely sat in front of him and he put his hands on my spine and with a very small movement put the 'tail', which was out of place back into its proper position.

'Now I am going to put on the heat,' he said.

I could feel waves of heat going up my back which vibrated all over my body. Only when he had finished did I realise it was his hands alone which had produced the heat!

From that moment on, my spine was in the correct place, but I had terrible adhesions of arthritis from the eighteen months in which I had been incapacitated.

Then, when I was thinking about the problem of arthritis, I read Adelle Davis' book which is now available in this country, called *Let's Get Well*.

She recommended for arthritis *calcium pantothenate*, which is a new way of taking pantothenic acid. She says in her book that deficiencies in this vitamin produce fatigue, listlessness, digestive disturbances, headaches, irritability, heaviness, mental depression, quarrelsomeness and recurring respiratory infections. She also said that calcium pantothenate removed the pain and stiffness of arthritis.

This was something I had never heard of before, so I

range round the Health Movement to find where I could buy some.

I found a firm who sent me tablets which contained 500 mg each. Within a few days of taking four of these tablets of calcium pantothenate a day, the pain was disappearing so quickly that I could hardly believe it! Then I learnt it was possible to have injections, which two doctors had been using for a long time.

I prefer injections, and it only meant having three the first two weeks, two the third week and one the fourth week. But for people who find it difficult to get a nurse to give them, the 500 mg tablets are miraculous. It means having to take four of them a day.

Everyone to whom I have recommended this remedy has been over-whelmed with the results.

Recent scientific findings show that arthritis is caused by a deficiency of pantothenic acid. Osteoarthritis in dogs, especially among pedigree animals, has been increasing during the last ten to fifteen years, and is probably due to these animals being fed on highly processed canned foods.

Pigs fed on a pantothenic-acid-deficient diet became extremely thin and emaciated, and have a rough coat with loss of hair. They also develop what has come to be called 'goose-stepping gait' in their hind legs which is due to osteoarthritis in their leg joints.

Doctors achieved the most remarkable results with vegetarian arthritics. When patients were injected with a mixture of royal jelly and calcium pantothenate they all showed a rapid disappearance of symptoms in fourteen days, with remarkable increase in the blood pantothenic acid level.

Another doctor has said that if pregnant women were given a daily supply of 50 mg of pantothenic acid, they would not only prevent a miscarriage, but their children would be born strong and many of the ills, physical and mental, from which the human race suffers would be a thing of the past.

Arthritis, whether rheumatoid or osteoarthritis, is on the increase the world over, and there is no doubt that it is due to the world population eating more and more of the highly preserved foods which we in the Health Movement are well aware are dangerous.

It is an insidious disease and may take many years before visible symptoms appear. We are all of us eating some pantothenic acid in our diet, inadequate though these amounts may be, but anyone who feels any twinges of pain — which means practically everybody in this country — from rheumatism, gout, or any other allied disease would be wise to take immediately at least 50 mg of pantothenic acid a day.

What helped me may not cure everyone. I have been particularly lucky, but the research done by the two doctors I previously mentioned shows that for a large majority calcium pantothenate has proved to be quite fantastic.

That is why I feel that here is a note of hope for the millions of people all over the world who are in pain from arthritis.

It is always exciting to find something new in the Health Movement, especially when one is up against arthritis, which is admitted by the doctors to be one of the most difficult diseases for which there is no real cure.

Where arthritis is concerned, every patient is different, and a great number do not respond to everything that has been suggested, including *Seatone*, which is acknowledged as being one of the best products, or even *Devil's Claw*, or *Calcium Pantothenate*.

Remember I fell down in front of the Taj Mahal and spent two years trying to cure the painful arthritis, which I did when I discovered Calcium Pantothenate tablets (500 mg).

Injections and tablets took away the pain, but the other day disaster struck! For the second time I put out my back, and it was only set in place when I called on the services of that great Healer, Major Bruce MacManaway.

I was however left with acute and very painful arthritis particularly at the points of the shoulders, across the back of the neck and down the base of the spine, which meant I found it difficult to walk.

I therefore returned to my beloved Calcium Pantothenate with, I regret to say, not the same results as before. In fact, this was a different sort of arthritis.

For me the doctors' palliatives are fatal, because if I am

tranquillized, even by one aspirin, I am unable to dictate my books of which I expect to do 6,000 to 7,000 words a day, and everything comes to a standstill.

Fortunately Mr Michael Van Straten came to my rescue by producing something I had never heard of before, but which has been much-tested and acclaimed in Switzerland, and is called *Magnetic Foil*.

This is a revolutionary new form of therapy available to us in this country at about £9.84p a pack. It comes in the form of an *Energy Pak*, containing bright gold magnetic foil, which is quite easy to apply to any part of the body.

The moment Michael Van straten applied it I had no more pain in my legs, which up until then had been agony when I wanted to walk.

I am told that muscle tension, which is common amongst long-distance drivers has responded magnificently to this treatment, so much so that Niki Lauda, the world-famous racing driver, used the foil after breaking his wrist, and was racing again three days later.

As you can imagine, two hours of speeds of up to 200 mph within inches of death is enough to make anyone tense, and Niki Lauda says that the foil relieves his tension in a fantastic manner.

All you have to do is buy the Energy Pak and follow the instructions which are quite clear.

Place the magnetic foil on any part of your body that requires it. The only difficulty is — and it is the only one — you cannot lie for long in a hot bath without the foil becoming detached, so it is better to shower, if you have one, while it is applied.

Having put the foils on the places where you need them you leave them on for up to seven days. You then remove them, leave them off for six days, then reapply if necessary with the adhesive supplied with the pack.

One pack will last you nearly a year and it is only when the foil begins to crack that you need another one.

The foil does not lose its magnetism, so you can use it many times.

All I can say is that when I use magnetic foil on my neck I have no more pain.

I have read clinical tests where patients who have been wearing neck-collars for years have been able to discard them.

The Priests of Ancient Egypt and the physicians in antiquity such as Hippocrates and Galen and, in the Middle Ages, Paracelsus, all reported amazing benefits to various ailments by using magnetic foils.

Now a great deal of research has shown how efficient magnetic foils can be in the treatment of fractures and arthrosis, besides being useful in healing scars, skin sores, joint pains, bruises, varicose ulcers and inflamed areas of the body.

Up until now such treatment required the patient to spend many hours in hospital with machines which created the necessary magnetic force.

Now you can treat yourself at home, easily and effectively.

Just as I am writing this, a new product has appeared which to me is a miracle, and it is called D.L.P.A.375.

D.L.P.A. is not a painkiller, it simply protects and strengthens our own endorphins which are the natural, built-in painkillers inside our bodies, and which were only discovered in the last ten years.

After a few days of using D.L.P.A.375 relief is often substantial, but if not, then continue for three weeks.

D.L.P.A.375 works for most people in this time, and its effect may be so prolonged that tablets are not needed for two to three weeks between courses.

For those who do not get relief with the normal amount, the quantity may be doubled to give D.L.P.A.375 its maximum chance of success.

DL-Phenylalanine is a mixture of the two forms of the natural amino-acid Phenylalanine (PA.) The body uses PA in the metabolism and it is therefore not a drug. Like vitamins, we get amino-acids all the time in our food, but imbalances occur because of the extensive use of synthetic processes in food production.

D.L.P.A. should *not* be taken by people with Phenylketoneuria, or during pregnancy.

CHILDREN AND VITAMINS

When my three children were small they all suffered with hereditary Eczema, so they learnt when they were very young self-control where food was concerned.

They soon found that chocolate, soft drinks, citrus fruits and white sugar in any form made their Eczema worse, and they knew if they ate those things they would suffer for it.

It is very important for children to understand that the right food and of course vitamins help them, but it has taken a long time before the manufacturers realised that small children find it difficult to swallow, and therefore they should have chewable vitamins.

These we now have, and my small grandchildren like them very much because they are based on honey. They like chewing *Dolomite* tablets, although personally I think they are rather unpleasant unless one swallows them. They also enjoy chewing *Acerola* (Vitamin C) tablets, and will take them eagerly. In fact when they were very little they used to call them 'Granny's Sweeties'.

One of the most fantastic vitamins which has helped mothers all over the world is *Vitamin B6*. It was first discovered in America, when it was found that children who suffered from 'tantrums' and were considered to be out of control were really just vitamin-deficient.

So if your child is 'difficult', give him Vitamin B6, which we have now in Chewables, and you will see a difference immediately.

Also, one of the most sensible things for children, which keeps them calm and also gives them perfect teeth and strong bones is Bone Meal, which you can buy in tablet form.

What an expectant mother eats and drinks affects her baby all through its life, and it is satisfying to think that so many mothers today are beginning to understand that pre-natal care is as important to their children as what they do after they are born.

I recommend to every mother who writes to me when she is pregnant that, as soon as her baby is born, first of all to give it honey, just a tiny half-teaspoonful in its bottle of water.

Secondly, as soon as it can take solids, crush up a Bone Meal or Dolomite tablet, and give it either with the food or again in a little honey.

Honey is essential for children, and should be continued to be taken by adults all through their lives. It has a good effect on children's growing capacity and on its health, and again prevents any form of nerves, which often results in bed-wetting.

Honey strengthens the bladder, and a teaspoonful before they clean their teeth makes them sleep peacefully and eliminates all nervous afflictions.

I believe that the greatest happiness for a woman is to give birth to children, to love them and to receive their love, in that it makes her a complete woman.

NOTE

A new book which will be of tremendous help to women concerned with the effect of different additives on their children and themselves is called *E for Additives* by Maurice Hanssen with Jill Marsden and is published by Thorsons. It has everything you should know about the additives in your food. I found it very, very helpful.

WATCH YOUR CIRCULATION

People often forget that essential to our health is our circulatory system. In fact, without it we become vegetables, immobile and undoubtedly miserable.

One circulatory disorder, arterio-sclerosis, is one of the main causes of death in the Western Hemisphere. It is estimated that 900,000 people die of this disease in America alone each year.

Arterio-sclerosis is known better as 'hardening of the arteries', and Leon Chaitow, who is an expert on these matters says that the causes are: diet, lack of exercise, and stress.

It is very difficult for any of us in these troublesome and distressing days not to suffer from stress, but I have found that vitamins, especially B6 and the Indian Ginseng, do help stress tremendously.

So what we have to consider is whether we take enough exercise and if our diet is right.

As we know, most people's diet is completely wrong, so it always sounds to me like *Alice in Wonderland* that we have to take pure food in the form of vitamins that we would otherwise be able to put into our mouths, if everything was perfect — which it is not!

One of the pure foods that I can thoroughly recommend for circulatory problems is a combination of some magical substances brought out by the Cantassium Company, and which is called *Cardeymin*.

Each tablet contains 250 mg of B.13 and Magnesium, 50 mg of B.13 and Potassium, and 75 mg of bromelaine.

Dr Nieper has found that six of these taken every day in treating Angina and Coronary Heart Disease has had a sensational effect on the number of patients on which he tested it. In fact, one test on seventy-six patients of which twenty had been expected to die, resulted in only two.

Of course, if one is dealing with circulatory conditions, it is extremely important to take enough Vitamin E.

I believe that Vitamin E is the nearest thing we have to life, and it carries oxygen all over the body, reduces cholesterol, assists blood flow to the heart, and contains in it the anti-clotting factor.

I think every man and woman of any age needs Vitamin E, but especially when they are getting to the age when they might have hardening of the arteries.

The food to avoid if you have any sign of hardening of the arteries is of course:

1. All refined carbohydrates: white flour, rice, pasta of any description.
2. All sugar products.
3. Salt.
4. Oils and fats, except for a small amount of unsaturated vegetable oil.
5. Not too much animal protein.
6. Cows' milk.

I find that people are very ignorant about the latter, and I have discovered that cows' milk is almost entirely responsible for the enormous amount of glandular fever which young people suffer from in this country.

Needless to say, fresh vegetables and fresh fruit are very important and besides Cardeymin and Vitamin E, I think everybody needs Vitamin C.

B6 is also essential because of stress, and we are only just beginning to realise that the dangers people warn us about in Vitamin A were mostly mythical, and Vitamin A is not only a protection against cancer, but essential for a man's sex life.

Watch your circulation, and you will be watching yourself keep young, active and happy, whatever age there may be on your Birth Certificate!

WATCH YOUR EYES

I receive quite a number of letters from men and women who are developing cataracts and who wish to avoid having the operation; also from people who work under fluorescent lighting, which is very bad for the eyes.

For the latter, I always tell them to feed their eyes all the time, and it is no use waiting until they start to hurt, burn, or feel gritty before they do anyting.

I talked about this problem to Dr Leonard Mervyn, who is the brilliant Scientist at Healthcraft's, and he has now put together all the essential vitamins for the eyes. This will be a tremendous help to everybody when they work hard, and are getting on in years.

Our eyes are so precious that we often forget to pay as much attention to them as we do to the other parts of our face, and even our hands.

I had a little trouble with one of my eyes two years ago, and it made me very, very careful about my sight. It also made me think of what I could do to keep my eyesight strong and healthy.

Eyebright, which has now been introduced into the Health Movement, carries in each tablet all the essential vitamins.

Every tablet you take contains Calcium Phosphate, Eyebright extract, Maize Starch, Riboflavin which is Vitamin B2, and in my opinion absolutely essential for strong eyesight, also Vitamin A and Vitamin D.

There are various other ingredients, but these are the main ones, and if you take three tablets with each meal you will feel an immediate improvement in your eyes.

For those who are getting really old, or have eye trouble, they can increase the number of tablets they take.

QUINTESSEN

Some years ago when I was working with Jimmy Lee-Richardson in the Health Movement, he decided to put on the market an essence which contained all the rarest plants, exotic fruits, herbs and minerals from all over the world.

He sent people thousands of miles researching for what was one of the most unique and natural food supplements ever introduced by the Health Movement.

For a year or so *Quintessen* has not been obtainable, but now it is back, and I know the people who have written to me asking for it because they have hay fever will be delighted.

For some reason which we do not really understand, one of the ingredients is a remedy for the attacks of hay fever which beset so many children and adults in the pollen season.

I have not found it to be a cure, but if you take Quintessen first thing in the morning, and again in the afternoon, it prevents all the tiresome effects of this allergy which comes from pollen.

Apart from this, Quintessen is a 'pick-me-up' after illness, and a marvellous daily supplement for those who want to feel really well.

Naturally, it is delicious, which is not surprising, when it contains so many exotic and mouth-watering fruits.

Many of the contents had never been appreciated except by a native population who had known for centuries that the plants and fruits grown in their particular country helped their men, women and children to avoid illness, and be healed if they contracted one.

As you can imagine, Quintessen is therefore unique and, what to my mind is important, it also contains the natural minerals and amino acids which we all need.

THE MIRACLE STRESS PILL G.E. B6

It would be impossible for us not to realise that, with the terrible anxieties which beset us as a nation at the moment, the majority of adults are suffering from mental strain.

The economical situation, inflation, the increasing price rises, and the anxiety over houses, families and a thousand other things make every man and woman a prey to what we call 'stress'.

This is something which affects us both mentally and physically, and unfortunately the medical profession has no cure but to prescribe in most cases the tranquillizers which, as the Kennedy report showed, made people worse, and are both addictive and dangerous.

I think everybody knows now that tranquillizers and sleeping draughts rot the brain and in some cases, after they have been taken indiscriminately, reduce the patient to a mental case.

I am appalled that we are becoming in this country nothing more or less than a nation of drug-takers.

For some years now I have been helping people by advising them to take G.E.B6 and I have found that this particular combination makes people feel happy. If you feel happy, then the world is a better place, not only for yourself, but for everybody with whom you come in contact.

I persuaded the Scientific Laboratory at Healthcrafts to produce my magical formula in one capsule! This makes it perfect for men who say they will take one capsule or tablet only, and no more — then dash off to the office!

All you have to remember is to put a capsule by your husband's place at breakfast and take our own at the same time. Then forget about your health for twenty-four hours with the knowledge that you will feel extremely well, happy and full of self-confidence.

The 'Stress Pill', as I call it — or G.E.B6 — is to my mind one of the most exciting products we have in the Health

Movement, and I have hundreds of letters from people who tell me so.

Let me tell you first about *Ginseng*, although you may know a lot about it already. It first appeared in written form in the First Century BC and was also mentioned in the ancient Atherva Veda of India.

In 1974, Father Jartoux, a missionary for many years among the Chinese, wrote a whole book on Ginseng.

The Chinese consider Ginseng the supreme remedy for any sort of sexual inadequacy, and the finest grades of Chinese Ginseng were reputed to have the power to restore fertility, even to those who have long passed the normal child-bearing age.

The Ancient Greeks spoke of Ginseng as an important ingredient in love philtres, but all this knowledge was kept in the East, and it was only about fifteen years ago, when I was in Hong Kong, that I first heard about Ginseng.

It was then terribly expensive, but prized, I was told, not only by the rich Chinese, but also by the very poor, who saved up to buy it, because they thought it made them well and prolonged life.

We are told that Dr Kissinger took it in his exhaustive flights all over the world and the last Astronauts that went from America to the moon were told it was a compulsory part of their diet, as it prevents 'jet-lag', and sharpens the brain.

Travellers in China, from Marco Polo onward, have been extremely impressed with the virility of the Chinese men of advanced years, and the Chinese themselves readily admit that it is partly the use of Ginseng which is responsible.

The Russians are enthusiastic about Ginseng. When I was in Leningrad some years ago, the scientists were working on the brain and they told me that when Ginseng was combined with B15 the results were fantastic.

It is always difficult to estimate the physical effect of herbal medicine on people, but however much Ginseng may be disparaged, I am convinced, like the Chinese, that it has a magical ingredient which our bodies and minds need.

Now, I am pleased to tell you, Ginseng is available in all

our Health Stores.

I take Ginseng first thing in the morning, and I find I can do an enormous amount of work during the day, and still not feel exhausted in the evening, which at my age is remarkable.

There are no side-effects, and no doubt in my mind that it does not only make you feel well, but also that its name, which means 'All healing', is a correct one.

The next ingredient is *Vitamin E*, which I call the '*Love, Life and Sex*' Vitamin, because it supplies us with all those things, besides being a prevention and cure for diseases of the heart.

Because it carries oxygen all over the body it is excellent for the circulation, and the fact that put externally on a scar it will remove every trace of it in time, shows its amazing healing qualities.

The last, and very important, ingredient in the 'Stress Pill' is *Vitamin B6*. It wsas assumed for years that we get all the B6 we need in our diets, until recently when it has been discovered that the majority of people are now deficient in this very important vitamin.

Hospital patients given a diet adequate except for Vitamin B6 developed mental depression, sore mouths, lips and tongues, and in time insomnia, extreme weakness, nervousness, dizziness, nausea and vomiting.

The strangest abnormality however was eczema, which appeared first in the scalp and eyebrows, around the nose and behind the ears. When Vitamin B6 was given to these patients, their conditions quickly became normal.

HORMONE REPLACEMENT TREATMENT

I was delighted and at the same time once again in the position of being able to say 'I told you so!' when it was announced that Doctor Peter Layde, Director of the US Centre for Disease Control in Atlanta, Georgia, had, on a special project, found that women who use the contraceptive pill are less likely to develop cancer of the womb or ovary.

The reason for this is because the combination pill contains oestrogen and progesterone. I have fought for over ten years for women at the 'Change of Life' to be given *Hormone Replacement Treatment*.

It all started when I read a book written in 1966 by Doctor Robert Wilson, Consultant in Gynaecology in three of the most famous hospitals in America. He said that after experimenting with 5,000 patients he found that those to whom he had given oestrogen during the menopause looked and felt younger, and kept their figures and their sexual feelings up to a very old age.

He also said that where women suffered from a deficiency of oestrogen, which happens to us all when we reach the 'Change of Life', they withered inside, became old, more prone to disease, and in many case found it hard to make love.

'The skin of the breasts coarsens,' he said, 'and becomes wrinkled, while women often lose their erotic sensitivity and sometimes do not even respond to pain stimuli. Only timely oestrogen replacement therapy can prevent this premature decline of a woman's symbol of femininity.'

After reading this book I started to fight for British women to be allowed to have Hormone Replacement Treatment, especially when I discovered that four out of five women in the United States were having it, and other countries were following their example.

Only in England did the doctors say that the menopause was a 'natural occurrence' and women were left sometimes to suffer very severely through what is a very difficult time in their lives.

A few years later Wendy Cooper came along with her book called *No Change*. She travelled all over the world and studied what was happening in other countries. She found that, as far as Hormone Replacement Treatment was concerned, we were so behind everybody else in medical science that it was quite shaming.

With Wendy Cooper I went on a number of television and radio programmes, and wrote numerous articles.

It is entirely due to our fight that today there are Menopausal and Hormone Replacement Clinics all over the country. All the great London hospitals have them as well as those in the North, Birmingham, Durham, Brighton, and dozens of other towns.

In fact, there is no reason why every woman during the 'Change' should not be able to go to a hospital clinic, if her doctor is so old-fashioned that he will not prescribe Hormone Replacement Treatment.

In the Health Movement we specially recommend three natural hormones which are: *Premarin*, *Progynova*, and *Harmogen*.

I take Premarin and find, as do so many other women who write to me, that the results are sensational! It makes all the difference to our health and fitness, as well as to our love-life.

Fairly recently a number of doctors in this country started to say, for no reason as far as I can ascertain, that too much oestrogen may cause cancer, and a great number of women were very worried by this statement.

From my long experience I was convinced that they were wrong and were merely taking up an attitude which could confuse and upset those who had benefited so immensely by oestrogen.

But a survey made in Georgia showed that the two cancers which kill more than 4,000 women a year in Britain are twice as common amongst those who do *not* take the 'pill', as those who have taken it.

The authors of this study which involved 3,200 women at eight different US centres say they consider the effects of the 'pill' could have a large public health impact, saving many lives.

They compared the 'pill' in a study with two large control groups and found the women who were cancer-free were those who were on the 'pill'. They also stated that, for cancer of the womb, the best protection is provided by the combination pill containing oestrogen and progesterone.

Dr Peter Layde ended his statement by saying that as in the past there had been a lot of concern about the 'pill', some justified and some not, this is very reassuring news for women who use oral contraception.

These findings are to be published in the Journal of the American Medical Association, but in the meantime I wanted to tell you what has already been said to prevent there being any more fears amongst women in taking Hormone Replacement Treatment.

The difference it makes is so spectacular that I feel terribly upset when women write to me and say they are not going to take it, or that their doctors will not allow them to.

Some of the first symptoms one gets when one is over forty and in need of oestrogen is a thinning of the hair and what is always described as 'nerves'. Oestrogen also *prevents* acceleration of the pains, aches and diseases to which we have a personal tendency and often become very upsetting during the Change.

I am now eighty-three, and I could not be without my Premarin, which, as I have had an hysterectomy, I can take every day without the pause which is essential for those who still have a period.

It makes all the difference to my feeling of well-being, keeps my skin soft, supple and comparatively unlined.

It has also been acknowledged by the medical profession that if you take oestrogen you very seldom have a fracture or break a limb!

In layman's language, oestrogen 'keeps the juice in the bones' and, in even simpler terms, keeps us young!

If your doctor refuses to give you H.R.T. for a really good reason and not because he feels it is old-fashioned or anything like that, I should first of all get a second opinion from one of the Clinics, otherwise I can recommend two things which will help you.

Some people really cannot take Hormones and now in Austria they have been using Melbrosia P.L.D. which is a combination of Pollen and Royal Jelly. An increasing number of women who take this remedy prove that this natural product can rank high in the treatment of the climacteric syndrome.

It was found after thirty days of taking Melbrosia P.L.D. that the typical complaints of hot flushes, insomnia, weak concentration, etc., were all reduced and the remarkable thing about it is that the women regained their vitality and mental balance to an amazing degree.

Alternatively there is Ladycare No. 2 by Healthcrafts containing our old friend Vitamin E which is known to help with hot flushes, headaches and the distressing itching associated with the menopause. It also contains another old friend, Vitamin B6, which alleviates the depression which can result at this time. There are also Vitamins A and C, which are important in building up resistance to illness and infection.

The decreased production of sex hormones is known to cause a loss of Calcium, and Ladycare No. 2 contains an adequate daily supply of this mineral and Vitamin D which aids the absorbtion of Calcium.

These tablets should be taken daily throughout the month, especially in the morning with food. I have seen tremendous results from both Ladycare and Melbrosia P.L.D., but I prefer, where possible, for women to take natural hormones which work immediately.

BE WISE IN HOSPITAL

A doctor friend of mine who had worked both in England and America once told me that the difference between the two countries was that, despite our surgery being the best in the world, hospitalisation in America is fantastic and patients there are given vitamins both orally and by injections, and every effort is made to have them 'fighting fit' before they have an actual operation.

His comments have been born out by an International Symposium on vitamins which states that, in Europe at least, any person going into hospital for more than two weeks can expect to come out worse off in their nutritional state than when they went in, mainly due to a combination of hospital food and the effects of medicinal drugs.

A recent study carried out in Leeds General Hospital on two hundred patients who went into hospital for minor surgery showed that over 60 per cent of them were mildly deficient in vitamins and minerals.

Antibiotics can cause depletion of the essential intestinal bacteria with adverse effects. Taking ample 'B' Group vitamins will help them restore themselves, and lactobacillus acidophilus can be replaced in tablet, capsule or powder form. I recommend High-Comp. Vitamin B.

One of the more important aspects of nutrition arises when a patient is to undergo surgery, or is admitted to hospital with injuries. The rate of healing of any wound depends on a good nutritional status. Of prime importance are Zinc, Vitamin C, Vitamin A, Vitamin E and of course Vitamin B2. It is now becoming standard practice in some surgery units to give patients Zinc and Vitamin C in particular before surgery, and after it, to ensure that the most efficient healing can take place.

I was asked by somebody who was going into hospital what she should take *before* she went in, while she was actually in hospital, and when she came out.

I advised her to take a multi-vitamin tablet which should balance the body by giving it everything needed in the way of both vitamins and minerals. I always recommend Gev-E-

Tabs and two of those should provide the average person with everything they require.

I also suggested she took either Indian Ginseng or G.E.B6 (the 'Stress' pill) which contains Ginseng, Vitamin E and Vitamin B6 together. However, if you are having an operation, you do need extra Vitamin B6.

When I was in hospital I took Vitamin C, which is the best healer in the world with the exception of the new *Selenium* which unfortunately did not exist then. Selenium has been found to have fantastic healing properties and is essential as a prevention for cancer and heart attacks. It also gives improved virility and quick healing in every case.

The research on Selenium has been going on all over the world and some American scientists now contend that its use can reduce breast cancer by 80 per cent of its present level. So when you go into hospital take two Selenium ACE every day; it will give you 150 micrograms of this fantastic mineral.

There are two problems one comes up against in hospital; one is that they always try to give you sleeping pills, and these you must fight against taking at all costs.

If you do what I did when I went into hospital you will sleep peacefully without the aid of sleeping pills. I took honey and cider vinegar. You must take this with four Dolomite tablets or Bone Meal tablets in a tumbler of water, last thing at night, and you will sleep peacefully.

The other problem which confronts all hospital patients after an operation is constipation. Here again, the hospitals have still not got around to recommending Bran, even after one has had an operation for Diverticulitis, as I did. Bran is absolutely essential for everybody, every day of their lives, but especially when you have had an operation.

There is one more vitamin which is absolutely essential which is Vitamin E which carries oxygen to every part of the body. This is what you want, especially after an operation, and if by any chance you have one like I had for the intestines, then you must have Lactose Propolis Capsules.

This has been found to be a fantastic healer for anything to do with Colitis, gastric troubles or anything else to do with the intestines.

I am appalled at the food in almost all of the hospitals I visit. They give everybody thick black China tea, white bread, which is extremely bad for you, as is white sugar.

If you really care about getting back to life, take with you honey instead of sugar, and if you want to sprinkle it on your food buy raw sugar from a Health Shop, or Grape Sugar. Better still, however, is Glucose.

Try to arrange for your visitors to bring you, if you want bread, Wholemeal Stone Ground bread from the Health Shop, although bread is unnecessary if you are inactive and not taking any exercise.

Lastly, try to arrange to have your own tea, which should be Ginseng Tea. This is an energiser, healer and a stimulant all in one, and very much better for you than the coarse black tea which is universal in every hospital.

Take your vitamins every day, despite the fact that the hospital staff will tell you they will do you no good, and like me you will come bouncing back to health far quicker than anybody expected, and of course you must go on taking them when you are home again.

As a last thought, do remember that you can, by prayer and thought, link up with a Power that is more effective and stronger than anything produced in any hospital.

Pray for good health, believe that you will have it, and I am certain, whatever happens, God will not fail you.

A MIRACLE INGREDIENT: LECITHIN

Lecithin is something which has only just come to the notice of a great number of people, but it does in fact concern us all and is of paramount importance to good health.

Lecithin occurs both in plants, animals and human beings and it is present in all the cells and organs of the human body. This makes it essential to life, because none of our cells and organs can function without its presence.

In a healthy person Lecithin forms 30 per cent of the dry weight of the brain, and 73 per cent of the total liver fat — both of which are greatly decreased in persons dying of heart disease.

Regular exercise increases the Lecithin content of muscles, and there is an increase of up to 25 per cent in the amount of Lecithin in the flight muscles of birds when they have been flying regularly.

Of course we know the old story that if the diet contains the right food the human body can produce Lecithin, but we are all aware of the difficulty of getting the right food.

It is quite obvious to me that we have now to add Lecithin to all the other essential pure foods that we take as supplements.

When, because of stress, physical or mental exertion, old age or a diet containing insufficient of the component parts required by the liver to produce Lecithin, there is a danger that the shortage can seriously affect our health. This is because the lack of Lecithin causing a build-up of cholesterol in the artery walls leads to arteriosclerosis: the cause of ischaemic heart disease.

The most exciting thing about Lecithin is that it definitely helps to prevent diseases of the heart. High blood cholesterol is, as we all know, one factor. Others are cigarette smoke and obesity, stress and high blood pressure. To combat these, large amounts of Lecithin are absolutely essential.

What will interest a great number of women is that

Specialists now recommend Lecithin for weight reduction.

Lecithin is a nutrient which has a major function in assisting the body to burn up fat. It not only burns it faster than anything else, but keeps moving the fats which accumulate, usually in the wrong places!

By keeping the fat broken down into small particles, Lecithin ensures that they cannot form deposits which of course is marvellous news for those who have 'a spare tyre'.

Needless to add, it is not as simple as it sounds, you have to watch your calories and carbohydrates as well!

The third way in which Lecithin can help, which is very important, is by preventing the retention of water.

I receive many letters from older people who have been put on those horrible diuretic pills prescribed by the doctors, and which invariably have side-effects!

The most popular one which is handed out for every possible complaint contains a very strong sedative, and should never be taken by anyone who is driving a car.

Lecithin however is a natural diuretic in that it helps to remove excess fluid from the body and, at the same time, will improve the function of your brain which to me is extremely important.

Lecithin is a preventative of gall-stones, and it is now thought that multiple sclerosis can be helped by the addition of it to the diet.

Let me return to the brain which is more important than anything else. The brain is oneself — the more it is depleted, depressed, or becomes ineffective with old age, the less we exist as a person.

I have tried the new Lecithin Plus Granules which Healthcrafts have put on the market. They come from Soya Flour, which is the best source of protein fortified with calcium and magnesium.

It tastes quite pleasant and it is suggested that one level tablespoonful is the right amount with each meal, or you can mix it with your bran at breakfast, or make it into an excellent drink.

This is prepared as follows:

1 tablespoon Lecithin
2 tablespoons Protein Powder
Put into a liquidiser with a little bran, add two cupsful of skimmed milk and a little egg.
Add a banana, an orange, or any other fruit that is available.
Blend for thirty seconds.

This produces a high protein drink which will give you a 'lift' whenever you feel down or lack energy.

It will keep for some time in a refrigerator.

MIGRAINE

I have been lucky in that I have never suffered from migraine, and I never have a headache. I am convinced this is because I eat properly and take vitamins. But many of my friends suffer agonisingly.

One friend of mine had this complaint so badly that the doctor treated him with some peculiar drug which landed him in hospital for a long time, suffering from the side-effects of the drug!

There is now a product which has been put together by some wise and clever people who have followed Preventive Medicine and who were aware that the yellow and green leaves of the Chrysanthemum plant are more effective than anything else in eliminating this distressing complaint.

The leaves have an extremely strong and characteristic aromatic odour when they are crushed. To avoid the bitter taste people have put them between bread and butter, or mixed the crushed leaves with honey. Others have even gone to the ingenious lengths of moulding their own pills with icing sugar.

Now it is so much easier to take Feverfew Tablets, by Healthcrafts, and the effect seems almost miraculous.

The tests on Feverfew have been very extensive, and 93 per cent of those who tested it had a condition which had been diagnosed by a doctor, a migraine clinic or a hospital's Out-Patients' Department. 77 per cent had never taken any other herbal remedy.

After trying Feverfew, one-third had no further migraine attacks while four-fifths of those who stopped taking it had a recurrence of severe migraine within a week or two.

It is interesting too that when the leaf was given to people suffering from arthritis it helped them, while others said they had less muscular tension and more restful sleep.

Several people have told me that Feverfew has helped them to be rid of depression and other nervous disorders. One was delighted at the excellent effect it had on her asthma.

In 1772, Dr John Hill in his book *The Family Herbal* says of Feverfew:

'In the worst headache this herb exceeds whatever else is known.'

Every day I find new evidence that the more we look back at the medicines recommended by Culpeper in the seventeenth century, we find they exceed in every way the doctors' chemical prescriptions which so often have terrifying side-effects.

A survey by a major Pharmaceutical Company showed that eight out of ten migraine sufferers buy 'over the counter' proprietary medicines to help them with their condition.

They also discovered, and it seems incredible, that 7–8 per cent of the adult population are migraine sufferers and the fact that they treat themselves indicates the lack of confidence that so many people are beginning to have in what is known as 'the doctor's pills'.

If you suffer from migraines or headaches I suggest you not only try Feverfew, which seems to me a wonderful way of relieving your suffering, but also make quite sure that the migraine does not come from your stomach, as I have found in so many cases.

I always advise anyone who says they are suffering from migraine to take Propolis Capsules, one or two every day, which will make sure that everything inside is working perfectly.

Another product to help migraine sufferers is alled 'Combination F' which has been produced by New Era Laboratories.

'Combination F' combines Kali, Phosphate, Magnesium Phosphate, Sodium Chloride and Silica, and has an excellent effect on anyone who is nervous and inclined to have migraines.

Headaches usually occur when the digestion is faulty, so try to make sure that you do not eat anything late at night that will disagree with you.

I find that many people as they grow older are unable to eat salads, and the last thing you want to do is to eat uncooked things at night which will keep you awake and which often results in a heaviness in the morning, causing a headache.

Do also remember that certain foods take longer to pass through the body than others. Veal, for instance, is a slow digester and so are a number of other things, which you should, unless you are young, have found out for yourself.

A number of people are allergic to certain foods. For instance, many are allergic to milk, although they often do not realise it.

I have found that migraines in most people come from stress, worry and as I have already said, bad eating. I always recommend that such sufferers keep off stodgy, starchy foods like pastry, white bread and of course white sugar. Try also to steer clear of fizzy drinks and chocolate.

Any migraine sufferer should keep away from anything sweet, except of course honey, which is completely harmless and also helps to soothe away the tension which is an inevitable part of any migraine or headache.

Take your Feverfew and remember there are thousands of other herbs ready to help us if we can only find them, or remember for what purpose they were used in the past.

PAINS IN THE HEAD

I have found that, if one has pains in the head, this usually comes from lack of circulation, and there are three things which are extremely effective, and will take away the pain.

One is called *Circu-caps*, and the other is Rutivite E, and the results of these two products are almost instantaneous.

The third is one I found amazingly effective. It is NEW ERA's COMBINATION F which has in it KALI PHOS, MAG PHOS, NAT MOR SILICA.

'BODY' MINERALS

I have always believed that minerals are important, but the difficulty has been in the past that no one has really researched to find out how much of the mineral we take is absorbed by our bodies into minerals already present.

Now a tremendous breakthrough has been achieved by Healthcrafts who have introduced to the market Chelated Minerals in a form which are exactly the same as those already inside us.

These Chelated Minerals, which I call 'Body Minerals' so that it is easier to remember them, are absolutely essential to our health, our character and our personality.

I am convinced that minerals keep us young and that Aminochel Minerals, which are really natural body minerals, will make an enormous difference to the construction of our bones, our blood and our looks.

AMINOCHEL IRON

This is the first of our Body Minerals and we all know iron is a component of haemoglobin, the pigment which gives the red colour to our blood.

'You must never forget, a doctor said to me, 'that Haemoglobin is a carrier of oxygen, and lack of iron means a reduced amount of oxygen being carried round your body.'

This is why people who are anaemic always feel tired, listless and suffer from headaches. One in every two women is in need of iron.

'I feel ghastly,' a mother with three small children told me.

I had one look at her skin and gums and knew she was extremely anaemic.

Ordinary iron tonic pills and tablets oppress the body mineral iron. This usually causes constipation and kills off vitamins in our bodies.

That is why these new Body iron tablets can make one feel wonderful and of course give extra energy.

AMINOCHEL CALCIUM

We all know that Calcium is a building material for bones and teeth, but what had not been realised until a short time ago is that Calcium, if we take enough of it, definitely keeps us young, particularly women who lose calcium at an alarming rate when they are over forty.

In women, bone density usually reaches a peak at thirty-four to forty-five years of age. Dr Albanese reports in the New York State Journal of Medicine. Then it begins to slide. Maximum density occurs in men about ten years later.

This, I feel, may be the reason why women of middle-age often look years older than their husbands.

But now new scientific research shows that if we can take enough calcium and it is absorbed into our bodies, then we can delay the ageing process and keep our whole body, especially our bones, much younger than our years.

Aminochel Calcium is the nearest supplement to milk calcium that has yet been produced, and milk, as we all know, is an excellent source of calcium. Unfortunately, in the last few years the National Herd — in other words, all the cows of the country — have produced milk which in many cases has been polluted by penicillin and other antibiotics which are used when the cows have mastitis.

AMINOCHEL MAGNESIUM

This acts on the nerves and is essential to prevent irritability, depression and bad temper. A nerve is usually surrounded by calcium and magnesium, and when a nerve is stimulated these minerals are replaced by sodium and potassium.

When the crisis is over the nerve returns to rest and calcium and magnesium move back to surround it. When these two things are deficient, which happens to a great number of people these days, the nerve stays in a state of excitement and you know as well as I do what the doctors recommend for this, and that is to give you tranquillizers, which make you worse, rot the brain and, where women are concerned, ruin their looks!

'I'm a mass of nerves,' a woman said despairingly last week, 'but my doctor just gives me drugs which make me feel awful!'

People with nervous conditions nearly always suffer from a lack of magnesium, and that is why this Aminochel Magnesium is extremely important to everyone in these difficult times.

AMINOCHEL ZINC

Zinc is found in the prostate and in the reproductive organs of both sexes. It is involved in every stage of the female reproductive process.

Zinc has been found to help tremendously in the prevention of prostate troubles and prevents hardening of the arteries and in treating certain forms of mental depression.

It is also absolutely wonderful for people who suffer from skin diseases, poor learning ability, slow wound-healing, and slow development of the sexual organs.

Many diseases and drugs lower the level of zinc in our bodies, and many women in particular who are on the contraceptive pill are deficient in zinc.

I am sure that this mineral will prove a real blessing to people who suffer from any of these things. I have found, personally, that by taking two 'Body' zinc tablets a day my skin is whiter and clearer. I am delighted!

AMINOCHEL COPPER

This is essential to prevent general weakness, impaired breathing, grey hair, lack of fertility, heart defects, digestive disturbances and anaemia.

It can be dangerous in very large amounts, but absorption of 'Body' copper is so effective that small doses are all that are required, and I think that many of us need copper very badly.

AMINOCHEL MANGANESE

This mineral should be used by anyone who suffers from

arthritic or rheumatic conditions. Normal ovarian and testicular functions depend on having enough manganese in our bodies.

A deficiency of this is quite frightening as it leads to a lack of sex interest, low fertility and unco-ordinated muscle movements. Very low levels of this mineral are found in people who are suffering from heart disease.

When-you think that one in two in America die of coronary thrombosis, one begins to wonder whether they are particularly lacking in manganese.

AMINOCHEL CHROMIUM

A deficiency of this mineral leads to high blood sugar, trouble with one's eyes, heart and circulatory troubles.

Yeast provides the best sort of chromium to be absorbed, but only tiny amounts are present. 'Body' Chromium is therefore important, especially in diabetes and pregnancy.

All these are a terrible amount for us to think of taking daily. Therefore, for the ordinary person, I recommend the MULTIMINERAL AMINOCHEL which contains a balanced proportion of the minerals I have mentioned, with and addition of Chelated Potassium, Iodine and Phosphorus.

I am taking at the moment two of these Multi Body Mineral tablets every day, and I must say I feel extremely well and find that my bones are stronger than they have been for some time.

What is so interesting is that the Health Movement is producing more and more products which are equated with the actual vitamins and minerals in our bodies so that they cannot do us anything but good.

Also the fact that they are chelated means that we are not wasting our money, and they are really absorbed.

Doctors and Scientists have said for years that minerals are important, but until now they have not been able to make the minerals work 100 per cent once they have entered the digestive system.

THE AMAZING ROYAL JELLY

When I wrote any book *The Magic of Honey*, which has sold millions of copies all over the world, I said that Honey had some miracle substance that no one has ever been able to completely analyse.

A lot of people told me this was nonsense, so I am delighted to find in the new research on Royal Jelly that, although the investigators have agreed that it has rejuvenating powers, no one knows why.

They in fact said: 'Royal Jelly obviously contains some other factors which science has not yet been able to detect.'

This, I believe, is the magic which Mohammed refers to when he says:

'Honey is the Medicine for the soul; benefit yourselves by the use of the *Koran* and Honey.'

Royal Jelly has been limping along behind the consumption of Honey for some years, but Ortis of Belgium are now bringing us fresh, pure Royal Jelly each week.

Customers can order weekly supply packs of 4 × 5 grams of *Api Fresh Royal Jelly* from their retailer. The order is then telephoned to the refrigerated depot, then despatched by first class post to reach the retailer the next working day.

Royal Jelly should be as fresh as possible because although Honey will keep for 3,000 years, as they found when they discovered some in a tomb in Egypt, and which was perfectly edible, I believe that fresh food is better than that which has been kept for a long time, however well it may taste.

Royal Jelly has existed since the beginning of time and yet this magical substance has still not been analysed, even though there have been some marvellous results over a five year investigation.

This research was done in Czechoslovakia by Dr Josef Vittek, Biologist, and Dr Jaroslav Kresanek, Pharmacologist, at the Medical School in Bratislava.

— They fed Royal Jelly in various amounts to test animals, and found that it speeded up their growth and increased their resistance to disease.

— Royal Jelly had an anti-bacterial and anti-virus action.

— Hens fed with Royal Jelly increased their egg-laying capacity 20–100 per cent.

— Royal Jelly accelerated the formation of bone tissue.

— Topical application of Royal Jelly helped to heal wounds in half the time.

Other experiments showed excellent results in the treatment of the diseases of ageing and the hardening of the arteries, and every researcher has agreed that Royal Jelly has a stimulating effect upon the functioning of all our various organs in the body.

We have a number of Royal Jelly capsules in the Health Movement — the one I have been taking regularly is Healthcrafts, which has 100 mg of Royal Jelly in each capsule. I think they are very invigorating, and my son finds they help his skin and his asthma.

Bumbles Royal Gellee, which comes from Power Health Products contains 150 mg of the best Royal Jelly in each capsule. It comes in a handy little flat plastic case, which you can slip into your pocket and take to the office. It very particularly states that you should take your capsule before breakfast, but, knowing how difficult men are about taking vitamins, I don't worry what time of the day they take it, so long as they do!

PROPOLIS

Ray Hill has written an excellent book on Propolis which tells us how the bees that feed on honey mature within twenty-one to twenty-four days. The Queen Bee, who is fed on Royal Jelly, is fully grown in sixteen days.

What is more significant is that the Worker Bees live an average of two to six months, while the Queen Bee may live for as long as eight years. They certainly work the Queen Bee very hard, because all this time she is producing eggs. She lays about a quarter of a million of them each season, often more than 2,000 in a single day!

What the scientists find so fascinating is that since the Queen Bee and the Worker Bees are hatched from identical eggs, it is obvious that the only reason for her longevity, size and marvellous fertility is her food.

For hundreds of years scientists have been trying to find and identify the substances of this food, but so far their efforts have been unsuccessful, although every year they identify more vitamins, more enzymes and more proteins.

But the special magic still eludes them, and this is why I am quite certain that Honey, in all its various forms and derivations, is the food that God has given us for healing and for good health.

Honey has, since 400 BC been used on wounds and as a means of curing ulcers. Some years ago, a leading British Gynaecologist startled the medical world when he said he found Honey far superior to any drugs when dealing with wounds and any other infected conditions.

At the Norfolk and Norwich Hospital the surgeons use Honey on open wounds and have written many articles on the subject. Now that preventive medicine is coming into fashion, because of the terrible side-effects of so many anti-biotics and drugs which keep appearing on the market, honey is more in demand than it has ever been.

THE MAGICAL MINERAL: SELENIUM

It has been discovered that if we want to maintain good health, increase our resistance to disease and be certain of a long and energetic life, we need to take *Selenium*.

Most people have never heard of this essential mineral and it is only now, after an enormous amount of research by Scientists in America, that its importance has been realised.

Selenium is in the soil, but modern fertilisation and the endless chemicals poured onto the land have reduced the Selenium content even in areas where the soil once contained enough of this vital element.

Selenium was first spoken of as a prevention against cancer, and American Scientists now contend that it can reduce breast cancer to 80 per cent of its present level. They have also proved that, where there is little or no Selenium in the soil, there is more cancer and more heart disease.

Selenium, they have shown, protects animals from developing cancer, and added to the diet of cancer-prone patients has improved them enormously.

The heart muscles require Selenium, and animals deficient in Selenium develop heart disease very similar to humans.

It has also been proved, and I find this very important, that Selenium supplements reduce the damage incurred after heart attacks, and helps to regulate the blood pressure, and quite a number of people have told me, too, that when they are taking Selenium it reduces heart pain.

It is also very significant to learn that Selenium is essential in reproduction, for without Selenium we find not only infertility, but also a depression of sexual vitality and drive.

The Americans, who do their investigations very thoroughly, and spend a great deal of money on them, have discovered that the birth rates in the United States are directly proportional to the level of Selenium in the diet, and this, of course, adds up to the fact that if you have enough Selenium you live longer and remain younger than you do without it.

No one wants to linger on to a senseless, miserable old age when you are an encumbrance to everybody you know, and Selenium, without a doubt, keeps you youthful and active, and gives you the joy of living which we all seek.

Besides being in the soil there is of course some Selenium in our food, but it is almost impossible to obtain enough every day. In fact for ordinary healthy people, the daily requirement is 150 micrograms, while the prevent or help any of the diseases I have mentioned, you need 200–300 micrograms.

Foods which generally contain Selenium are: meat, chicken, lamb, pork, fish, shell-fish, grains, cereals, fruits and vegetables.

But, as so often with a special mineral, one would have to eat a great deal more of these foods than one usually does to get the right amount of Selenium to keep well and to give one that extra youthful drive.

It is therefore much easier to take one or two Selenium tablets a day, depending on their strength.

It is however absolutely essential to look at the label on the Selenium packet in your Health Store to make quite certain that the Selenium is one with Yeast. It is not only more effective when combined with Yeast, but safer from creating any toxic condition.

Another very important addition to Selenium is Vitamin E.

The inter-relationship between Selenium and Vitamin E has been found to have a beneficial effect on people who wish to have a baby and, what is more, in a low Selenium area, there has been higher infant mortality.

Selenium is now being considered for hens in order to increase egg production.

When all the various clinical tests are brought together, it is obvious to me that we should be very stupid if we did not realise the tremendous importance of Selenium plus yeast plus Vitamin E.

Fortunately, there are now quite a number of Selenium products in the Health Stores, and I take two Selenium ACE a day, which contain 50 micrograms each.

Having recommended the same to somebody as old as myself with a bad leg ulcer, I am pleased to report that the ulcer has now shrunk and grows smaller every day.

As one specialist said:

'It seems inconceivable that any single nutrient could perform the near miracles described by dozens of reports in the technical literature.'

TO SUMMARISE SELENIUM:

1. Helps prevent heart disease and cancer.
2. Slows down the ageing process.
3. Protects against various eye problems.
4. Relieves fatigue and boosts energy levels.
5. Is essential to sexual functions.

SLEEP, BLESSED SLEEP

I was talking to a very distinguished Peer the other day at lunch and I was proclaiming against the horrors of tranquillizers and sleeping pills when he said to me, 'Look at my wife. Mogadon seems to agree with her.'

I looked at his wife who I have known for a long time and realised that, while she was in her fifties and still a pretty woman, she had the inevitable look of someone who takes these pernicious sleeping pills.

Her skin was very white but looked as though it had been dug out of a tomb. She had unnaturally deep lines under her eyes and down the side of her nose to her mouth and a criss-cross network at the sides of her eyes and on her forehead.

In other words she had the lines of a woman ten or fifteen years older than she was. This is the inevitable result of sleeping pills, apart from the fact that sooner or later the brain is affected and you become slower and more stupid until one finally lands up as a kind of vegetable.

This is not an exaggeration. I have seen it happen over and over again, and many of us will remember how shocked we were at the last pictures of the wonderful Sir Winston Churchill when he came to the window with his wife. He looked vacant and almost like a moron.

This was the effect of being given a sleeping pill every night by his doctor which he vividly describes in his autobiography.

Therefore, most older people like myself have a horror of sleeping pills and tranquillizers which in our old age will render us senile that we become just a body to be carted around by our relations or nurses.

'What can I do to sleep?' people say plaintively. I have hundreds of letters each year saying how difficult they find it to get a good night.

Lack of relaxation comes from an over-active brain or the fact that one is not feeding the nerves of one's body properly.

There is actually no such thing as 'nerves' which is a term

that is over-used today. It is just malnutrition in a form which shows itself in us being on edge, irritable and often tearful over things which are not important.

The most essential vitamin to prevent this is of course *Vitamin B6*. I take, every morning with my other vitamins, two 100 mg tablets of B6 and it does help enormously to prevent stress of everyday life, from showing in one's reactions to difficulties, in other words bad temper.

When I go to bed, having dictated 7000 words, written inumerable letters and taken far more telephone calls than I can count, I often do feel it hard to 'switch off' and go to sleep.

What I do myself and what I advocate to other people is really very simple.

First of all I have my Honey drink. You must be aware by this time, as I have said it so often before, that Honey is a marvellous food given us by God, and is the only one which is not only a fantastic healer, but is also a sedative and an energiser.

Honey is now used by nearly every athlete and it will also surprisingly make you sleep.

I therefore take two large teaspoonfuls of Honey with a teaspoonful of Cider Vinegar in a tumbler of water and with it, and this is important, 4 *Dolomite tablets*. You can take *Bone Meal tablets* instead if you like, but the Calcium will definitely help you to relax and also gives you strong bones, teeth which do not decay, and improves your nails.

There is also something else which has just been found to be very important with regard to sleeping, and that is something called *Inositol* which is again a B Vitamin.

The best way to take this is in *Lecithin* which as we know is a protection against heart disease and also an aid to slimming because of its ability to work on the body's fat store.

Again, it is a nerve tonic and a revitalizer. There are various ways to take Lecithin which I have described to you before. The one I find most agreeable is *Vita Buerlecithin* and I take a tiny glass of this, the glass being supplied with the bottle. This again helps one to sleep.

In America there is a Chapel and a whole congregation of people devoted to healing through pressure points, and one of these can prove of immense benefit to non-sleepers.

High on your forehead where you would have a widow's peak there is a point which, if you press with the first finger of either hand, will make you yawn. This means you are relaxing.

Feel about for the actual point, and when you find it because it hurts a tiny bit, keep your finger on it and you will start yawning.

If you are still not sleepy, you will find two other pressure points on the tip of each shoulder. Again you will have to feel for them and when you find the place which hurts keep your finger on it until the pain goes and again you will find yourself yawning and beginning to feel sleepy.

A large number of people tell me that they read the last five pages of one of my books! I must admit that when I feel upset, or have had a row with somebody, or have so much work to do the next day that I cannot stop thinking about it, I do the same thing.

Read about love, the love I write about, which is of course spiritual and divine, and at the same time do not forget to say your prayers.

Prayer is a linking-up with the powers which give us sleep which is the greatest blessing to mankind.

During sleep we revitalize ourselves and also the healing process which takes place all over our body is accentuated during the night, especially if we have given our bodies the healing elixirs of Honey, Lecithin and other vitamins.

Remember, sleep is important to us all, and if possible we should have eight hours of it.

SLIMMING SENSIBLY

I have always refused to recommend slimming cures because I think they are dangerous.

I have seen so many examples of young girls with Anorexia Nervosa, having no idea as they slim and slim in a fanatical manner that they are ruining their future life, because in many cases they will be unable to have children.

The other day I met a man who had Anorexia Nervosa who had slimmed himself because he thought he would look younger. The result was that, while he had an abnormally thin body, his face was that of an old man, although he was not yet middle-aged.

What people fail to understand is that slimming can become like drug-taking, so that it is obsessive, and women go on and on trying to get thin, until they really make themselves ill.

The great example of this was one of the most beautiful women in the world, Elizabeth, Empress of Austria, who was the first woman in history we know of to have slimmed herself.

Because no one knew very much about slimming in those days, she slimmed in entirely the wrong way with the result that she had Oedema, which is a swollen stomach caused through malnutrition.

This is happening in a great many cases today, and the frightening thing about excessive slimming is that it affects the brain. Women become vague, stupid and show all the first signs of degenerative ageing.

Now, at last, I have discovered something I can wholeheartedly recommend and which really works.

The other day Sir John Mills, who is a very old friend, and his brilliant playwright wife Mary came to lunch with me.

He had just come back from India, where he had been working on the film on Gandhi in which he plays the part of the Viceroy. He told me he was seventy-five and I said to him:

'John, you have a wonderful figure, and unlike most men

of your age you have no paunch. Do you take a lot of exercise?'

He replied:

'I am much too busy, but I will tell you my secret, which I have just revealed in my autobiography *Up in the Clouds, Gentlemen, Please*.'

In this delightful and amusing book he tells how in 1937 he had a very bad ulcer. He was put on a boring diet of milk and misery which is all the doctors can suggest, even today, for Duodenal Ulcers.

He says himself:

'I seemed to be making no improvement whatsoever. I still suffered from the pain in my duodenum, but, what was worse, my brain seemed to be about as alert as one of the boiled eggs which I consumed by the dozen.'

He was then told by his sister about a book published in America and written by a doctor called William Hay, and after he had read it he went on the 'Hay Diet'.

Dr Hay believed we have two digestive juices, one for the starchy foods and the other digests the proteins. He believed that if we crammed the stomach with starch and protein *at the same time* we created indigestion, which develops into acidity, and once the system becomes acid instead of alkaline, any of the diseases we are prone to find a breeding ground to grow in.

The diet is therefore easy — you eat all your proteins at one meal and all the starches at another.

What is so interesting to slimmers is that the Hay Diet takes off weight and inches on the body where one wants it, and from my point of view as a hostess, and also somebody who enjoys good fod, it is a joy.

I can eat everything I am offered at lunch or dinner except for the pudding course. At tea, if I wish, I can enjoy chocolate cake and anything else that is starchy, but I have found that if you keep to the Hay Diet, you seem to lose your craving for sweet things.

I always take honey at night and often in the morning, so I get all the sweetness I need then.

Sir John told me that however much he eats and drinks, as long as he keeps to the Hay Diet, he never gains a single ounce.

He certainly looks marvellous and as he is not very tall it would be disastrous if he got fat.

I have recommended this diet to many of my friends who are extremely impressed by it, and I now recommend it to you.

To those who prefer to try crash diets which are really dangerous to your health, to your body and to your mind, let me add that citrus fruits are much too strong for the stomach and pit the soft flesh inside, often with disastrous results.

Milk, which is another slimming food advocated by many experts is, in my opinion, absolutely wrong for adults, and I have discovered over the years that milk is one of the foods that gives young people especially glandular fever.

If you have once had glandular fever, whether as a child or a teenager, you should never drink milk again, as it is undoubtedly a carrier of this disease.

I am also against the type of slimming foods which swell up your inside to make you feel as though you have had a good meal when in fact you have had nothing of any nutritive value. This again can lead to very dangerous side-effects and so can the continual taking of Diuretics.

Most diuretics are made from chemicals and they remove the essential Potassium from our bodies. Although scientists have seen the danger, and one or two products now contain this mineral, it is synthetic, while in the Health Movement it is a natural product.

This is called '*Aquatrim*', which will not hurt you in any way if you increase the dose to obtain the right result. However, if you take Bran, then you will find that you do not need a very strong diuretic.

Remember that in removing the water from your body the first thing that suffers is your face, because the reason you have an unlined face is due to the water contained under the skin which prevents lines and wrinkles from forming.

I have studied slimming for a long time simply because so many people write to ask me what they can do to lose weight so that they will look beautiful on the beach, etc.

etc., and I can assure you that this is the first time I have ever been able to say that here is something that will take weight off, but slowly and without affecting your face.

The obsession with women to be slim is an entirely modern one and you should remember that it is not so much what you look like but what you are in yourself, and I have found that most men prefer 'a handful'.

A doctor in America came out with a revolutionary announcement some time ago that people who were a little overweight from a modern standpoint, were better-tempered, more philosophical about life, and more charming, so to be certain that in taking away those few extra pounds you are not depleting yourself of your '*joie de vivre*'.

STOP SMOKING!

When I was the Chairman at a Foyle's Luncheon for Jimmy Young recently, having proposed the Royal Toast, I added:

'And now you may smoke — if you want to kill yourself!'

Everybody laughed, and yet I was saying something so true that it is frightening!

Lung Cancer is the third worst type of cancer we have threatening us at the moment, and is the most common malignancy in the United States and Western Europe.

You are *five times* more likely to get Lung Cancer if you smoke, and even if *you* do not, you are *three times* more likely to get this pernicious disease simply by being in close proximity to those who do smoke, whether it is at home, in offices or in trains.

When I try to warn people about the effects of smoking they say:

'I've got to die of something!'

That's all very well, but they are not only killing themselves but all the other people with whom they come in contact.

Today scientists are working hard to find a cure for this dreadful scourge, and they have discovered that the risk of developing Lung Cancer, even among cigarette smokers, is less among men who eat large amounts of carrots, spinach, and other vegetables that contain *Beta-Carotene*.

According to a spokesman for the National Cancer Institute in Bethesda, this new discovery indicates that a diet high in *Beta-Carotene* (a form of Vitamin A), contributes to a more than 40 per cent chance of decreasing the risk of developing certain types of cancers.

The study, which has been carried out over nineteen years by scientists in Norway, Japan, Singapore, the United States of America and Britain has recently been reported in *The Lancet*.

Today there is a large reduction of smoking amongst men, while women still smoke at all times of the day even, which I consider appalling bad manners, at the table at mealtimes.

What women will never admit is that if they smoke they smell, but I can smell if a woman smokes as soon as she enters a room. When smokers write to me, the writing-paper smells, and so does everything else they touch, which is why I will not employ in my house anybody who smokes.

I believe also that a woman's skin is affected not only in texture, but also in colour. I have a friend who was an acknowledged beauty with a fabulous white skin and red hair, but because she has smoked regularly over the years, her skin in now coarse like leather and has a distinct yellow tinge, while her hair is a dull, lifeless 'beige'.

Smoking is a habit, and people who smoke light up a cigarette without even thinking what they are doing.

We have seen on television the ghastly effect on an unborn baby whose mother smokes. And when a smoker comes in contact with a pregnant mother we can only ask ourselves — are we prepared to run the risk of an unborn baby becoming handicapped by strangers?

The whole problem is so fraught with dangers that I believe we should all of us bring pressure to bear to prevent smokers from increasing the horrors of Lung Cancer wherever they go.

Yet there is hope in the form of Carotene which is found in abundance in carrots, and it is also plentiful and sometimes in greater concentration in other vegetables, such as spinach, beet, greens, broccoli, kale, tomatoes and apples.

These vegetables also produce Vitamin A which helps us in the growth and repair of body tissue, and is essential for our eyes.

It is difficult to be sure these days of fresh vegetables unless one lives in the country, but Healthcraft's have now produced an excellent capsule called: '*Beta-Carotene*'.

They cost £3.25p for 90 capsules, which is not expensive when you think of the alternative of being unhealthy, especially if you smoke, and risk having that terrible, frightening disease for which the scientists have still not found a completely foolproof cure.

When my two sons went to Public School at the age of twelve I said to them:

'Education is very precious. It affects your whole life, so it would be a pity to waste it. If you smoke at school, you will be beaten; if you drink you will be expelled, but if you wish to do either of these two foolish things, then do it at home, and see how you get on.'

Having thought this over, they said:

'But it's no fun if we are allowed to.'

I replied:

'That is up to you.'

The result is that my sons have never smoked, and they never drink spirits, only wines, which to my mind is good teaching.

May I say again that anybody who is foolish enough to smoke must, after these new findings, try to have a diet which includes foods rich in Carotene.

Doctors say that for a smoker half a cup of carrots every day might possibly mean the difference between life and death.

I suggest if this is not possible it might be far more convenient to buy the *Beta-Carotene Capsules*.

WHAT THE DOCTOR ORDERED

I was shocked, but not surprised, to read the other day that tranquillizers can turn women into shop-lifters *without knowing it*. The last few words are really the most important.

Mr Geoffrey Norman, Secretary of the Magistrates' Association, has said that many defendants in police cases are probably affected by drugs without their knowledge.

This to me is horrifying in an era when we are supposed to be intelligent enough to determine our own lives, and live in a free democracy.

For the last seven years I have been fighting a continuous crusade against sedatives and tranquillizers. On every radio programme and practically every television show in which I take part, I tell people, because I think it is so important, that these two things which are handed out by doctors destroy the brain.

Now we have been told that brain damage similar to that found in very heavy drinkers and alcoholics is being discovered in people who have taken the popular tranquillizer 'Valium' for long periods.

This is one of the world's commonly prescribed drugs, and is given out by doctors as if it was confetti.

Valium is violently addictive, and, as the Reports show, not only is one woman in five taking it in this country, and one man in ten, but it is also costing us as tax-payers £40,000,000 a year to supply that drug alone.

Some of you may have read about Freddie Starr, who took nearly three months to get rid of the hallucinations and obsessions he had after taking Valium, which had nearly ruined his career.

When I went to Russia, the Scientists in Leningrad confirmed my belief that tranquillizers rot the brain, and now at last nearly every newspaper in England has carried the message.

A close favourite of Valium is Librium, and I wonder how many of the twenty million people who swallow these are aware that the manufacturers state in their literature that they should not take alcohol whilst on these drugs?

I have never met anyone yet who has been given this information, nor are they told that the side-effects may include shop-lifting, or that they should *not* drive a car?

Brain scans on a small group of twenty patients who have been taking Valium for five to ten years show evidence of cerebral atrophy and brain shrinkage among other signs of damage.

Professor Malcolm Lader, Professor of Psychopharmacology at the Institute of Psychiatry in London, who carried out this study says:

'We should take care in using tranquillizers for a long time.'

He also calculates that there are perhaps 250,000 people in Britain, and one million in the United States, who have taken this tranquillizer for more than seven years.

He adds:

'If our figures are extrapolated, this could mean there are 100,000 people in the United Kingdom with funny-looking brains.'

Personally, I think the word 'funny' is wrongly applied. It is not our bodies who are 'us', but our personality, our characters and the very fact of being alive comes from the brain.

I hope a large number of people saw the Kennedy Report on television about the dangers of sleeping-pills and tranquillizers, especially Valium, which was exactly what I have been saying for years.

I am sure many people thought I was exaggerating, and yet the Kennedy Report showed that withdrawal symptoms can be worse than if one is taking heroin, and addicts suffer from palpitations, delusions and weakening of the mental faculties.

The whole Report was so terrifying that I would like to have it repeated and repeated for those silly people who believe that drug-taking is easy to relinquish once you have taken it for a short time.

Some time ago, I had a letter from the mother of a girl of seventeen, who was worrying because she had to pass her 'A' level examinations, and the girl had been given tranquillizers. I cannot imagine anything more likely to ensure that she failed!

Everybody reacts differently to different foods, different environments and difficult emotional situations, and whilst I deprecate any form of tranquillizer, sedative or sleeping draught, I do see there may be occasions when a patient needs one.

At the same time, he or she should be informed exactly what the effects may be, once they have swallowed whatever it is they have been prescribed.

Even the most familiar tablets which are advertised all over the place and are on sale in every chemist-shop can have side-effects.

Aspirin, for example, can cause serious internal bleeding and over 7,000 people are taken to hospital every year with this condition. I was also surprised to learn recently that it can cause gout.

When I was a County Councillor for Hertfordshire, I was told that in Hatfield, one of the New Towns I represented, young women used to get up in the morning and take two aspirins to help them through the day! It was crazy, but no one seemed to worry about it.

Paracetamol, which is another favourite handed out by many doctors, can cause severe and even fatal liver damage if it is taken in excess.

Pain-killers are another enemy not only to your body, but also to happiness.

Distalgesic, which is heavily prescribed, has a depressing effect on the brain. It is even stronger when it is mixed with other depressants to the nervous system, including alcohol.

Even the manufacturers admit the drug 'may impair the patient's mental and physical reactions whilst driving or operating machinery' and 'psychological and physical dependence may rarely occur.'

I wonder how many people who take these little pillow-shaped tablets read the small print when they buy this drug? Other possible side-effects, again listed by the manufacturers, include dizziness and vomiting.

I could give you a list of half-a-dozen that produce such unpleasant side-effects, and it would be much better to remain with the original disease!

Penbritin (ampicillin) can produce, for instance, an intensely itchy rash, in fact there are very few tranquillizers that do not have side-effects. You may have read of a Psychiatrist who warned of patients going into a state of madness after the withdrawal of the sedative Heminebrin.

Make quite certain that what appears to be a mild treatment for some quite commonplace disorder does not contain sedatives. These might ultimately prove to be addictive, so that you will have great difficulty not only in getting rid of the side-effects, but also in giving them up.

If you have become addicted to drugs you need to take large doses of Vitamin B6 and really optimum doses of Vitamin C and E together, and if you are a bad case you will need to take them every four hours. If you do this, you will soon be back to normal.

When a doctor, either a National Health or a Private Physician, writes a prescription you are never told, unless you can understand the doctor's hieroglyphics, what you are taking.

If you are in hospital and ask you will be told that it is what the doctor ordered, which is no answer at all.

The average person is very ignorant about medicines, and, because when we are ill we are as helpless as little children, we trust the doctor and do not like to ask a lot of questions.

But after the revelations on Valium, which was called 'The Happy Pill', I believe patients should make a point of questioning everything they are prescribed.

Of the 10,000 letters I answer on health problems every year, a third of the writers say that tranquillizers have made them worse and they want to give them up, but can't. Others say pathetically that they cannot sleep without a sleeping-pill, but are afraid by taking them that they will become a 'vegetable'.

Elderly people may also have hallucinations and become hopelessly confused. Again I recommend Vitamin B6, plus C and E together.

Mogadon, which is the favourite of the sleeping-pills handed out by doctors, impares your driving ability and again you should never drink alcohol when taking them.

A recent British Medical Journal affirmed that people who take tranquillizers are more likely to have a road accident, which more often than not involves somebody else's car as well as your own, so you run the danger of killing some innocent driver, due to the fact that your brain is not completely under your control.

And a final warning — all tranquillizers, sedatives, antibiotics and sleeping-pills affect the sex urge!

People taking any of these drugs will find they are less capable of making love because just as their bodies are sedated, so are their emotional reactions.

TRAVEL WELL

There is at last a solution to all the problems of travel sickness, as well as pregnancy sickness, which I know will be a joy to everybody who has to suffer every time they ride in a car, go on a sea voyage or fly in a 'plane'.

This is called *'The Travel Well Pocket Pack'* by Healthcrafts, and contains twelve tablets costing only 65p, although I know most people would pay almost anything to keep well when travelling.

The Travel Well tablets are made of a combination of Vitamin B6, which I have proved a hundred times relieves the nausea of pregnancy, and herbs, which have been used over the centuries to cure sickness.

Unlike commercial drugs, of which I very much disapprove, this combination does not make you feel drowsy and arrive at your destination feeling half-witted, with a terrible headache the next day.

One of the more popular herbs to prevent the nausea and vomiting associated with motion is Roman Chamomile. It was found by the Ancient Egyptians to possess this quality and is used by all herbalists.

Another important herb is Meadowsweet. This attractive herb which grows by the sides of our streams and rivers not only prevents sickness, but relieves the discomforts of the stomach which, for some people, is even worse than the sickness.

The most effective herbal treatment for sickness from motion, which of course includes the sea, flying and motoring, in Ginger. This was first found to be beneficial by Gerard in 1597.

Now, after all these years, a report in *The Lancet* from the Brigham Young University in Utah, and the Mount Union College in Ohio, USA, has proved that Ginger's powdered root is superior in every way to modern drugs.

This delights me, because as you know, I am so suspicious of the drugs which are handed out without proper tests, with the result that they have disastrous side-effects which for many people can either ruin their holiday, or more important, a business trip.

Tests were done on thirty-six undergraduate men and women who were susceptible to motion sickness. They were blindfolded and placed in a tilting, rotating chair, then were given either powdered Ginger, a well-known, much-advertised travel sickness drug, or a harmless placebo. As all these were in capsule form, they were not aware of what they were receiving before being rotated in the chair.

Every fifteen seconds they were questioned as to their feelings about nausea and gastro-intestinal distress, and after six minutes the chair was stopped.

The result showed conclusively that Ginger in powdered form was enormously superior to the drug and the placebo. It was concluded by those doing the test that Ginger and the drug functioned at different places in their action in stopping nausea and gastro-intestinal distress, and the more natural approach of Ginger was very much more powerful.

This has convinced me that *Travel Well* is exactly what has been wanted, especially for those with children like mine, who when they were young were incessantly sick on long car journeys.

I will also give you a good tip which I have found very effective on my small grandchildren.

Just before they start a car journey, place a piece of adhesive tape behind their ears on the protruding bone which is where our balance lies. It is a tremendous help in preventing them from feeling sick in the back of a car.

I hate sitting in the back of a car for this very reason, especially a large one, but in future I intend to carry *Travel Well* with me, especially when I am abroad because then I often have to sit in the back rather than the front seat.

We can all think of times, whether it is at sea, in the air or on the road, when we have felt rather queasy and would give anything to ensure that we arrive at our destination feeling bright and in good health.

Vitamin B6 is one of the miracle vitamins which helps us in so many ways, and now that it is incorporated in the *Travel Well* tablets we have something which has been needed for a very long time to make life a little easier for us when travelling.

THE IMPORTANCE OF VITAMIN C

There has been a great deal of excitement about our old friend Vitamin C since Mrs Thatcher said she took it regularly. In fact I know of few people who are health-conscious who don't take Vitamin C, as every day we appeciate it more and realise it has great unknown qualities that have not yet come to light.

The story I am going to tell you now is absolutely true — a man of sixty-eight was diagnosed in September 1981 as having malignant bowel cancer. He was operated on and the cancer removed.

Two months later, having developed another, he refused to take conventional drugs but decided, upon the advice of his daughter, who had consulted our brilliant scientific adviser Dr Leonard Mervyn, to take Vitamin C Therapy. This was in December, 1981.

On Dr Mervyn's instructions the Vitamin C régime was 10 grams a day for the first three weeks, and this was gradually reduced over the months to 4 grams a day. The patient is now taking 2 grams a day.

He recently underwent an exploratory operation, and there was no evidence whatsoever of cancer.

Not only had the cancer in the bowel disappeared, but there was no further evidence of cancer cells spreading to the blood and the liver as they had before.

His diet over the year since December 1981 was simply Vitamin C, plus a high fibre diet, less meat than usual, and no tinned food.

This man is a musician, and is about to be awarded an Honorary Degree by the Irish University for his talent. He recently organised a Concert and the proceeds have bought a cancer scanner for the local hospital, which is his way of saying 'Thank you'.

To me, this is a very exciting story and also a very encouraging one. We all risk having cancer, and every day more and more of my friends are menaced by this terrifying disease, but we know that a remedy is within our reach and can be brought from any health shop.

If we take an ordinary amount of Vitamin C every day, we will build up a wall of defence not only against cancer, but also against colds and influenza.

The moment I have the slightest feeling of the beginning of a cold or a sore throat, I take 2 grams of *High Potency Vitamin C* by Healthcrafts every 4 hours and it is very important to remember to keep to this 4 hour cycle.

Vitamin C is, incidentally, a natural dietetic, and anyone who is putting on too much weight finds it far more useful and far better than any of the doctors' dietetics, which in many cases have very unfortunate side-effects.

It has been known for over thirty years that pregnant women need more Vitamin C than others, but I have yet to find that during pregnancy women are supplied with this information and told it is something they should take every day.

A good intake of Vitamin C has, like Vitamin E, great value in controlling threatened, spontaneous and habitual abortion.

In a Dublin University there was listed some years ago some of the conditions in which Vitamin C is in particular demand. As these are so numerous, I will name a few to which many people are addicted: peptic and duodenal ulcers, heart disease, bronchitis, asthma, lung infections, anaemia due to iron deficiency, rheumatic fever and rheumatoid arthritis.

I am greatly relieved to know that smoking has been banned in our overcrowded Underground trains because heavy smokers not only destroy the Vitamin C in their own bodies, thus risking endangering their own heart and lungs but through smoking also affect those near them.

I would like to see this same rule enforced in offices were people work in close proximity to each other, but in the meantime, by taking an extra amount of Vitamin C, non-smokers can at least afford themselves a little protection.

It is said that the majority of British working men get their Vitamin C from potatoes, but these should be fresh, not dehydrated, and the same thing applies to all vegetables, and remember, once you have opened the package the very small amount of Vitamin C which has been preserved dissipates within a few hours.

THE FABULOUS 'LIFE' VITAMIN: VITAMIN E

When the Marchioness of Salisbury asked me if I would help her to fill the lorry she was taking to Poland for the relief of the mothers and children who were almost starving I got in touch with Mr Maurice Hanssen, who is President of the Health Food Manufacturers' Association.

He managed in only four days to collect Health Foods to the approximate value of £5,000. It was a wonderful effort for which Lady Salisbury was exceedingly grateful.

I was delighted to find that amongst the vitamins sent was Vitamin E, the 'Life Vitamin' which is essential to prevent habitual abortion and the terrible signs of malnutrition which comes when pregnant mothers are not properly fed.

Every day more things are discovered about this vitamin. *The Lancet*, on August 7th, carried the first report that Vitamin E is now found to be essential for human blood.

This is a major breakthrough, although we in the Health Movement have known for a long time that Vitamin E improves the circulation and makes more oxygen available for every muscle and tissue in our bodies.

I have also found over the years that it helps backward children to grow, completely eliminates varicose veins and, when taken internally at the same time as it is applied to the skin, can remove scars completely.

Dr Leonard Mervyn has written an excellent book on what he calls 'The Vitality Vitamin', which explains all the things that Vitamin E can do, and I was interested in reading in an American book that Vitamin E can reverse the ageing process.

Linda Clark, the authoress, and one of America's most read health advisers, begs us not to be afraid of taking too much Vitamin E. She says, and she quotes the Professors who have been studying this vitamin for years, that Vitamin E can keep you slim, active and beautiful, if you take it in large enough quantities.

I agree with her in that it is also essential for male virility, and when people ask me what will help them conceive having tried everything the doctor has suggested, I achieve marvellous results by telling the prospective father as well as the mother to take Vitamin E, as well as several other essential vitamins and minerals.

As Dr Mervyn points out in his book, one can of course obtain Vitamin E from food, but it is really so much easier in this day and age, when we are all so busy, to take, as I do, one or perhaps two Healthcrafts *Super Vitamin E* 1,000 i.u. (International units) daily.

Vitamin E is essential for any form of heart trouble, and there are various brilliant books written on the subject by doctors and surgeons who have used it with amazing success.

If somebody has a slight stroke, Vitamin E can help bring back the movement of the limbs, and also improve the mind.

Another benefit from Vitamin E was to a friend of mine, an attractive Russian Prince, who had an operation for cancer of the tongue. He was completely cured, but told me he had lost his sense of taste. I suggested Vitamin E which he took for nearly a month before he told me that his sense of taste had returned.

Dr Mervyn quotes the case of a man who suffered from very bad sunburn over the whole of his back. In an attempt to test the effectiveness of *Vitamin E Ointment*, this was used to cover half the sunburnt area. The other half was left untreated. The following day there was no sign of sunburn on the treated side, while the untreated side was covered in huge blisters.

In fact, where burns are concerned, Vitamin E can be the means of saving thousands of people from disfiguration.

Diabetes is usually 'conquered' by the use of Insulin. Last year a friend told me that his wife was taking more and more Insulin every day, and he was worried about it.

I suggested that he gave his wife Vitamin E, and he range me up three days later to say that already the doctor was finding that she needed less Insulin and was feeling so much better in health that she could hardly believe it.

It was an Italian doctor who made the first monumental

findings concerning Vitamin E in relation to Diabetes and heart diseases, and his example is being followed by medical men all over the world.

For ordinary people, it is very reassuring to remember that prevention is better than cure, and if we take Vitamin E every day it will prevent so many of these horrible diseases which come upon us later in life.

There is no doubt at all that Vitamin E is essential for stress and old age. This has been proven in almost every country.

At the University of Montreal, their first experiments were done with rats, and Professor Selye who conducted the tests found that Vitamin E almost completely inhibited heart disease, made the kidneys normal, and prevented the symptoms of old age in a spectacular fashion.

It must be true, as I have always said, that Vitamin E is the 'Life Vitamin', and essential to us in a thousand different ways.

The latest finding — that it is essential for the human blood — is so conclusive, that we have only to ask ourselves can we be so stupid as not to take Vitamin E every day of our lives?

DIFFICULTY IN BECOMING PREGNANT

I have produced so many babies when doctors have despaired and the would-be parents themselves had given up hope.

The first case I had years and years ago was a couple who had been married for twelve years, and although the doctor said there was nothing physically wrong the children just did not arrive.

The most important thing is for *both* the husband and the wife to take vitamins, and within two months a baby was started, and they now have four children.

Do not worry, try to relax and enjoy making love. At the same time take the following:

- 2 Vitamin E (1,000 i.u.)
- 1 G.E.B6 (the 'Stress' pill)
- 4 Aminochel Zinc (this is essential for the husband)
- 2 Vitamin A (25,000 i.u.) (this is again essential for the husband)
- 4 Dolomite, morning and evening — which means the baby will be born with strong bones, and you will not lose your teeth when pregnant
- 4 Keitafo Banlon Tablets, morning and evening
- 1 Vitamin B6 (100 mg)

A NEW SOURCE OF ENERGY: OCTACOSANOL

With the stress and worries of modern existence so many people feel exhausted. Even athletes are asked to expend more and more energy in every branch of sport, and for a long time I have been trying to find a vitamin which will give us extra energy.

This applies not only to the old who inevitably feel tired after a certain age, but also to young people who often do too much without the right food to sustain them.

Now at last we have something magical which I find fantastic at eighty-three, and my friends of every age have already told me they have found it wonderful too.

Octacosanol is a natural food substance which is present in Wheat Germ.

In 1935 when I first learnt about Vitamin E it was used only for brood mares. It was realised in 1926 that Wheat Germ Oil seemed to improve the reproductive disturbances in cattle and similar effects were noted in humans eleven years later in 1937.

I discovered personally that Vitamin E prevented miscarriages and also made me feel extremely well during pregnancy. Psychologically, I was certain it had a very beneficial and beautiful effect upon the child. Mine were all outstandingly lovely!

It was after the war that Professor Thomas Kirk Cureton in America began his pioneering research into the effects of Wheat Germ Oil on the stamina, strength, reaction-time and cardio-muscular functions of human beings.

Before this, the research scientists had thought that in Vitamin E there was some unknown factor which was particularly beneficial. Professor Cureton concluded that the critical 'unknown factor' in Wheat Germ and Wheat Germ Oil was *Octacosanol*.

Since then, it has been discovered that this performs an amazingly energetic function — which means 'energy releasing' — and can have a fantastic effect on those who take it.

Professor Cureton carried out a series of forty-two physical training programmes on 894 men and women. The effect of taking *Octacosanol* was fantastic!

It has been proved that the effects of *Octacosanol* improve stamina reaction-time, and has been used by Underwater Demolition Team of the United States Marine Corps with the support of the entire US Navy.

While this is marvellous news for people doing strenuous athletics, I find that Octacosanol gives me new energy every day without creating tension of any sort, but merely a feeling of well-being and happiness.

It is important to realise that to gain a significant difference and a lasting one, the tablets should be taken for at least four to six weeks.

In other words, Octacosanol is an active energy-releasing agent which I feel we all need if we are either actively engaged on work which requires concentration, or in any form of physical activity. And most of all if we are nearing old age.

In improving strength and endurance, it also stimulates the transfer of oxygen from the blood to the muscles, strengthening them and preventing fatigue.

THE FIGHT AGAINST CORONARY HEART DISEASE

I want to tell you about a very important dietary supplement which has recently been introduced to the Health Market in the fight against Coronary Heart Disease.

Men who have desk jobs often take an enormous amount of very strenuous exercise at the week-ends and I think most wives and mothers worry over this, but now *MaxEPA* can make them relax.

MaxEPA is the result of two decades of research and development, and is made from specially selected fish limpid concentrates.

The clue to the unique benefits of fatty acids in fish came from the Greenland Eskimos because in them the Coronary Heart Disease is practically non-existent.

Their natural diet of fish and seal meat prevents them from having many diseases which are, unfortunately, well-known to Europeans, the most important being those of the heart.

The modern Western high-fat diet elevates the blood cholesterol, and we all have friends who are worried about their rising blood pressure, blood clotting, hardening of the arteries, and, eventually, the threat of coronary heart disease.

MaxEPA controls and prevents all these horrifying things, and is heartily recommended by the Cardiothoracic Unit at Sheffield's Northern General Hospital, one of the largest in the country, and by the Queen Elizabeth College in London.

Therefore, if you are worried about your husband, your son, your daughter, or anybody else taking very energetic exercise, do suggest that they take a few *MaxEPA* capsules every day.

It is so much easier to be safe than sorry.

THE YOUTH PILL: S.O.D.

Every Spring, however old we are, our thoughts seem to get younger, and we have the urge to try something new. Far too often, it is difficult to find anything new for our body to keep up with our mind.

I take a 'Youth Pill' — S.O.D. (Superoxide Dismutase) — which is remarkable. I am told it makes you look and feel up to twenty years younger by forming up the skin, smoothing out wrinkles, and giving extra energy, and there are no side-effects, as clinical reports by top doctors have proved.

At the National Institute of Ageing, which is a branch of the Government's National Institute of Health, Dr. Richard Cutler, who I have always admired for his well-balanced and cautious approach to 'cures' says:

'S.O.D. may turn into a major breakthrough in health and ageing. Our studies show its exciting findings, and it certainly looks as if it will play a role of retarding age and promoting a long life.'

Dr Martin Feldman, a very reliable leading New York neurologist and nutrition specialist says:

'It is an exciting and effective way to stay younger and feel better.'

He goes on to say that by eating good, nourishing food with daily supplements of S.O.D., 'you'll look much, much younger. It can make people in their forties look in their twenties, while people in their sixties will look more like in their early forties.'

Then he adds: 'People on S.O.D. can actually avoid having a face-lift, or it can delay the need for one, while within two or three weeks of taking it you will find an increased sense of well-being and will become fatigued less easily.'

He does accentuate again, and I think this is important, that you must make sure you eat a balanced, nutritious diet which includes plenty of fresh fruit and vegetables. This also means, I am quite sure, that you eliminate white sugar and white bread, and do not smoke or drink to excess.

There are so many people who think that by just adding

one thing to their diet and going against all other rules, they can get results. The truth is that you must help yourself, because there is no pill in the world which can succeed if you put too many obstacles in its way.

Dr Hans Kugler, an organic chemist and noted authority on nutrition says very clearly:

'It is a miracle compound. You can literally turn back the hands of time with this enzyme. It is one of the major breakthroughs of the last decade in medicine and health. *If you eat a high-quality diet,* follow good health practises and supplement your diet with S.O.D., you can definitely look and feel years younger than your age — up to thirty years younger.'

A great number of other respected and admired scientists, physicians and authorities all agree that S.O.D. is a 'Youth Pill'.

Dr Richard Brennan of Houston says:

'Within weeks of taking S.O.D. people being to feel healthier and younger. Within a month or two they'll start looking younger, their skin will have better colour, and their bodies will start becoming trimmer and more youthful. The lines and wrinkles of their faces will begin to disappear.'

He finishes by saying: 'I have used it on over 1,000 patients. It is very definitely an anti-ageing substance that slows down degenerative diseases.'

To me, this is very exciting, and certain one is not taking a 'step in the dark' when one feels very enthusiastic and optimistic that after years of trying, they really have discovered a 'Youth Pill'.

ALL IN ONE: VITA YOUTH AND LIBIDEX 5

I have been teased so much by the National Press because I take so many vitamins that I welcome with joy 'combination' products, and although I tell the Press that at eighty-three I work very hard, they still pull my leg.

I am therefore delighted that there is a new product called VITA YOUTH which combines all the wonderful youth-giving ingredients which I have been writing about lately.

First of all VITA YOUTH contains S.O.D. (Superoxide Dismutase), which really does seem to take twenty years off one's age, and makes one feel so well, besides being unusually active.

It also contains R.N.A., and D.N.A., which like S.O.D. prevents the degeneration of the cells in our bodies which causes ageing.

Our bodies are made up of millions of cells, each one having a life of approximately two years. Prior to a cell dying, it reproduces itself. However, with each successive reproduction, the cell changes and deteriorates, so, as the cells deteriorate with time, this is when we notice that we are getting old.

Extensive research over many years has shown that the degeneration of cells can be rejuvenated by using R.N.A., and D.N.A. In fact in most people, new cell production ceases completely without these two vital substances.

As well as these marvellous cell rejuvenators, VITA YOUTH also contains SELENIUM and, as I have said before, wherever there is Selenium in the soil, there is practically no cancer, not heart disease, and people live to a great age.

The last product found in this formula is Vitamin E, which carries oxygen to every muscle in the body, particularly the heart. Vitamin E defends us against viruses and infections, and I have had such tremendous results with it on people who have suffered a slight stroke. Vitamin E has brought them quickly back to normal.

This vitamin also prevents and cures varicose veins. It also prevents miscarriages and every woman having a baby should take it.

It is recommended that one takes two tablets of VITA YOUTH every day and you will notice the results after approximately two to three weeks.

Another 'combination' which is having a huge success, and which is especially for adults, is LIBIDEX 5. This combines Siberian Ginseng, which impressed me greatly when I went to Russia, where they use only their own Ginseng, and in fact, Vladimir Lyakhiv took Siberian Ginseng during his record-breaking flight in the Soyuz 6 Spaceship.

LIBIDEX 5 also contains Vitamin E and Selenium, besides Zinc, which is essential for both men and women, as it ensures the proper growth and development of the reproductive organs, and the normal functioning of the prostate gland in men.

Recent studies show conclusively that Zinc deficiency causes sterility and dwarfism in humans.

Muira Puama is also found in this capsule, which although is not so well-known in the West, has been used by the Brazilians since time immemorial, and is reputed in Brazil to be one of the most powerful virility stimulants.

Certainly everybody who has taken LIBIDEX 5 tells me how well they feel, and how much it has contributed to their love-life.

And what could be more important to us all than LOVE!